Mary Senior Clark, Horace Harral

The Lost Legends of the Nursery Songs

Mary Senior Clark, Horace Harral

The Lost Legends of the Nursery Songs

ISBN/EAN: 9783744767583

Printed in Europe, USA, Canada, Australia, Japan

Cover: Foto ©Andreas Hilbeck / pixelio.de

More available books at **www.hansebooks.com**

Frontispiece.   HUSH-A-BYE BABY.

THE LOST LEGENDS

OF THE

NURSERY SONGS.

BY

MARY SENIOR CLARK.

ILLUSTRATED FROM THE AUTHOR'S DESIGNS.

LONDON:

BELL AND DALDY, YORK STREET, COVENT GARDEN.

1870.

LONDON: PRINTED BY WILLIAM CLOWES AND SONS,
STAMFORD STREET AND CHARING CROSS.

CONTENTS.

		PAGE
I. BO-PEEP		I
	Illustration by A. A. HUNT.	
II. PUSSY-CAT		19
	Illustration by G. H. GARRAWAY.	
III. JACK AND GILL		31
	Illustration by R. NEWCOMBE.	
IV. HICKORY DICKORY DOCK		46
	Illustration by A. A. HUNT.	
V. LITTLE BOY BLUE		54
	Illustration by A. A. HUNT.	
VI. TO MARKET TO MARKET		63
	Illustration by A. A. HUNT.	
VII. HARK, HARK! THE DOGS DO BARK		81
	Illustration by R. NEWCOMBE.	
VIII. DIDDLEDY-DIDDLEDY-DUMPTY		101
	Illustration by R. NEWCOMBE.	
IX. SEE-SAW MARGERY DAW		125
	Illustration by R. NEWCOMBE	

CONTENTS.

PAGE

X. BAA-BAA BLACK SHEEP 145
  Illustration by R. NEWCOMBE.

XI. BYE BABY BUNTING 174
  Illustration by R. NEWCOMBE.

XII. DAPPLE-GREY 197
  Illustration by A. A. HUNT.

XIII. RIDE A COCK-HORSE 208
  Illustration by R. NEWCOMBE.

XIV. HUSH-A-BYE-BABY 211
  Illustration by A. A. HUNT. (*Frontispiece.*)

XV. THE OLD WOMAN WHO LIVED IN A SHOE . . 220
  Illustration by R. NEWCOMBE.

XVI. A MONARCH'S DAUGHTER 236
  Illustration by R. NEWCOMBE.

JACK FROST COMING TO BO-PEEP'S ASSISTANCE.

THE LOST LEGENDS OF THE NURSERY SONGS.

I.—BO-PEEP.

> " I have a little sister, they call her Bo-peep,
> She wades through the waters, deep, deep ;
> She climbs through the heavens, high, high :
> Poor little sister,—she has but one eye."

IN a cottage on the borders of a wood there lived two children, a boy and a girl, with their father, the Wizard of the Wold. He was the descendant of a long race of wizards, and he looked hardly like a human being, with his dark eyebrows and black fierce eyes and long sharp teeth. The children, however, were not so strange looking, for their mother had been an ordinary woman, who married the wizard because he promised to revenge her upon some people who had done her wrong. But she did not live long, although long enough to repent of her marriage with so wild and uncanny a being.

The boy Cosmo was indeed dark-browed and silent, like his father ; but little Stella was merrier and more child-like, and had bright yellow hair, which was always flying about over her face and shoulders. They never went to school, or learnt to read and write as other children do ; nevertheless they had their lessons. Their father taught them the language of the birds and beasts, the winds and clouds, the trees and flowers ; and he made them learn by heart spells which enabled them to stop and question the wind as he went by, or to call the insects out of their holes to play with them. He encouraged them, too, in all manner of pranks, so that they would gather daisy-buds and make them grow and blossom on oak-trees ; or they would change birds' eggs, and make the thrush hatch wild ducklings, or the wren blackbirds. Sometimes they made cunning snares to trip the feet of unwary travellers, or would frighten them by making a snake suddenly wriggle across the pathway. And when their mischievous joke succeeded, they would clap their hands and run laughing away, for they had never been taught what was right and what was wrong. Only Stella sometimes thought she would rather not have robbed the little bird of her eggs, or the squirrel of his store of nuts ; and whenever Cosmo brought home small animals that he had hurt in what he called his play, she would tend and feed them until they were quite well, and then let them go free again. So it came to pass that all creatures learnt to love Stella, as much as they feared and hated her father and brother. Travellers used generally to avoid the road that led past the wizard's cottage, for it soon became known that people seldom passed that way without meeting with some mishap or other. But the bolder ones, who still ventured to take that road, used to give Stella the nickname of Bo-peep, because of the way she had of peeping out at them from the doorway, with her yellow hair blowing about her face, and hiding and peeping out again if they stayed to look at her. But if her father caught her at it, he scolded her and sent her to bed, for he would not let his children have anything to do with other people.

How the wizard employed his time, nobody knew. He read a great deal out of great black-letter books, and sometimes he would disappear for two or three days, and then come back looking just as black and sullen as when he started. Sometimes Cosmo wanted to go too, but the wizard never would take him.

"Father," said little Stella, one day, on his return from one of these excursions, "I have been wanting you. There is something that you have never taught me. I want to learn the language of the angels."

"What do you know about angels?" said her father, gruffly.

"I don't know anything," replied Stella. "I cannot see them; but the trees see them, for they bend their heads and hush the whispering of their leaves when the angels pass. And the clouds see them, for they part and make a gateway for the angels to fly through to the blue sky. I want to be able to see them too, father."

The wizard made no answer, and she was going on, "Won't you teach me——" when he turned and said: "I won't teach you anything—get along with you!" so angrily, that Stella ran away out of the house for fear of him.

It was a beautiful night ; and as she stood looking up at the stars, she thought that they must be the homes where the angels lived, and longed to go and live there too. Then she thought what wonderful beings they must be, that her wise father, who knew almost everything, should not know their language. Then she thought that they might be watching her now, though she could not see them, and a feeling as if of fear came over her, and she ran into the house again, away from the starlight.

It was not long after this that the wizard went off again, as he had often done before ; but instead of coming home at the end of a few days at most, week after week went by and he did not return. Perhaps, cunning as he was, he had met at last with some accident ; or, perhaps, he had grown tired of taking charge of his children, and was gone to settle somewhere else all alone. Be that as it may, he had disappeared, and Cosmo and Stella never saw him again.

They were not very sorry to lose him ; he had been too selfish and unkind for that to be possible. Cosmo, indeed, was glad ; for now, he thought, he would go and join himself with other boys—a thing his father had never allowed—and would be a little king over them, because of his knowledge of magic and power to work spells. Accordingly, the next time he heard boys' voices in the wood, he went out, and found a whole company of them bird-catching. Then Cosmo called, and a quantity of little birds came fluttering into his hands, and, laden with these proofs of his power, he went up to the other boys, smiling, and offering himself as their companion. But as soon as the boys saw him, they cried—" The wizard ! the wizard !" and, leaving nets and snares, they scampered away, never stopping to look behind until they were out of the wood. Cosmo flung down his poor little prisoners in a rage, and went home and sulked for the rest of the day.

" Those boys are stupid, ignorant fellows," he said to himself; "it was a mistake to begin with them. I will go to the town, and see whether the learned and clever men there will not perceive my superiority, and be thankful to have me for a companion."

But as soon as he entered the town some one recognized him as the boy who had done him and his fellow-townsmen so many an ill-turn as they passed along the woodland path : the news soon spread, and in a few minutes half the boys in the town turned out to meet Cosmo, and pelted and hooted him for a wizard all down the street and along the road towards the wood.

This time Cosmo went to bed and stayed there for three days, and when he got up he went about as black and silent as his father. He would hardly answer Stella when she spoke to him, and his only pleasure seemed to be to lay plans to annoy and hurt every one that came in his way.

One day Stella heard a cry of distress not far from the house, and suspecting that it must be some one whom Cosmo had played some trick upon, she ran out to see. There, in the ditch beside the path, lay an old woman dressed in her best red shawl and check apron, with a squashy, greasy mess under her that had once been a basketful of butter and eggs.

On helping her up, Stella was glad to find that the old woman was not much hurt, though so much shaken and frightened that she could not go on to market. Stella took her into the house and washed the dirt off her, and persuaded her to lie down on her bed, where the old woman fell asleep. She did not wake until it was too late to go home, and she agreed to spend the night at the cottage. When Cosmo peeped in and saw a guest there, he frowned fiercely, and went straight to his own room ; nor would he open the door when Stella presently came knocking to offer him some supper. But the old woman was charmed to find the little witch-girl so much kinder than she expected, and the next morning she said to her :

" My dear, it grieves me to think such a kind-hearted little girl as you have shown yourself to be, should yet be living in the midst of so much that is wrong."

" What does wrong mean ?" asked Stella.

" Whatever is displeasing to God is wrong," replied the old woman. Then seeing that Stella still looked puzzled, she added. " To Him who made us, and who is Lord of every-thing."

" Is he Lord over the angels ?" asked Stella.

" Surely," said the old woman. " They are his messengers, you know."

Stella had many more questions to ask, which the old woman answered as best she could, until at last she got up and said she ought to be going. Then, to her surprise, Stella put into her hands her old market-basket, neatly mended, and inside it were some plovers' eggs, and some large pieces of honey-comb.

"I put that in instead of butter," said Stella.

"My dear, this is worth a great deal more than my butter and eggs were," said the old woman. "I will come and see you again when next I pass; but if ever I can be of any use to you, only let me know, and I shall be very glad to help you."

The old woman had left Stella plenty to think about, with her new ideas of what was right and wrong. She began to fear to do anything that she felt not to be right, lest the angels, or the Lord of the angels, should be looking at her; and she tried to talk to Cosmo about it, but he soon cut her short. So while Stella was always looking upwards and thinking about what was good, Cosmo's eyes were always fixed on the earth, and his mind filled with what was bad; and he grew ever blacker and gloomier, until one day he too went out and did not come back again, and so Stella was left alone.

At first Stella wandered through the wood day after day, looking for him; but when she had convinced herself that he was not there, she went back to their cottage: for she said, "Surely he will come home at last, and if I wait here I shall see him."

One day she had wandered a little way into the wood to gather a few herbs for her dinner, when she saw two carrion crows before her, busy with a dead rat in the pathway. At the slight rustling which she made among the branches, one of the crows half rose, fluttering as if afraid; but the other cried with a hoarse croaking laugh, "What are you frightened at, you foolish fellow? there is no one here to be afraid of now. The Wizard of the Wold is gone, and his son is gone; there is nobody left but Bo-peep, as they call her, and she never hurts any one."

Now Stella understood the language of birds, so when she heard this she stopped to listen, hoping that she might perhaps learn something.

"Cosmo gone too, is he?" said the younger crow.

"And gone to a place which he won't get away from in a hurry," replied the elder.

"Where is that?" asked the other, while Stella listened with all her ears.

"Where is he, do you ask?" said the elder crow. "He is with the Black Dog, in the swamp!"

And both the crows left off eating, and nodded their heads at one another, by which Stella knew that it was something very dreadful.

"He is come to that, is he?" said the younger crow at last. "And what will become of him, I wonder?"

"That is what I have been wondering," said the other. "You know, if he were an ordinary mortal he would die before long in the Black Dog's service, and if he were wholly a wizard he would grow blacker and wilder, and his hair and teeth would grow longer, until he too would become a black dog, and then the two would fight until one remained the master of the swamp. But Cosmo is neither man nor wizard, so I cannot tell what will become of him."

"I suppose it is possible that somebody may go and save him?" said the younger crow.

"I don't, then," croaked the other. "Who would do it, I wonder? Why, everybody hates him; even his sister must, for he has behaved to her lately more as if he were a black dog already than a brother. And if she wished to do it, she would not know how."

"Who does know?" said the younger crow.

"Only three people in the world."

"Tell me who they are?"

Stella crept a little nearer, that she might be sure to hear the answer.

"First, there's the Wizard of the Wold," began the old crow, "and he is gone off nobody knows where. Then there's his brother, the Wizard of the Waste. And lastly, there is the Witch of the Willow-bank. They are the only three that know the secret how the Black Dog can be killed."

"Where does the Wizard of the Waste live?" asked the younger crow.

"Over yonder brown mountain, and far away on the other side," replied the other. But he lives in a hole in the ground, and no one knows the path to it except the caterpillar on the ragwort-stem; so he is safe enough from visitors. Ah, you thief, you! While I have been talking you have eaten up all the best bits!"

And the two crows fell to fighting over their carrion. But Stella had heard enough.

"I will go to the Wizard of the Waste," she said. "He is

my uncle, he will surely tell me the secret, and if it be possible for a weak girl to do so, I will save poor Cosmo, though I die for it."

She crossed the brown mountain, and reached the waste on the other side, and her body grew faint and her feet grew weary, but still her heart was brave. There were many ragworts on the waste; and she wandered long from one to another before she found the one on which the caterpillar lived. At last she spied, on a tall ragwort-stem, a brown, hairy caterpillar, with orange spots.

"Oh, caterpillar," said Stella, "tell me the way to the dwelling of the Wizard of the Waste?"

But the caterpillar shook his head lazily from side to side, and would not answer her until she threatened to force him by a spell. Then he said: "First a ragwort, then a burdock, then a ragwort, then a burdock, and so on to the end."

"That is not enough to guide me," said Stella. "How shall I know when I am there? for I see no house or hut on all this waste."

"You will get there," replied the caterpillar. "I only wish I were as sure that you would tumble in before you saw where you were."

"Thank you for nothing," said Stella, and went on her way from ragwort to burdock across the waste, until suddenly she saw at her very feet a hole in the turf, and rocky steps that led down into darkness. "This must be the place," thought she, and boldly clambered down.

There was a low cave at the bottom, and as soon as her

eyes got accustomed to the darkness she saw the wizard, crouching in a corner.

"Oh, Wizard of the Waste," she said, "my brother is taken captive by the Black Dog. Tell me the way to go to him, and how to fight with him, that I may set my brother free."

"You could not do it," said the wizard, after looking at her for some time. "He would kill you."

"I should not mind that," said Stella, "if I can save my brother;" and she went on for some time, persuading the wizard to tell her. At last he said, "What will you give me? I do not tell for nothing."

"Alas!" said Stella, "what have I to give?"

"Give me your witch-power and knowledge of spells," said the wizard. "My memory is failing, and your knowledge would make it fresh again."

"But how can I save my brother without this power?" said Stella.

"It will not help you," replied the wizard; "do not think of it. It would rather be a hindrance."

"Here, take it, then," returned Stella; "and now tell me what to do."

"Go to the Witch of the Willow-bank," said the wizard. "She will tell you. I have forgotten."

"Oh, but that is not fair," cried Stella. "Either tell me what I ask, or give me back my powers."

"I cannot talk any more," said the Wizard of the Waste, "it makes my jaws ache."

"Tell me at least how to find the witch," entreated Stella.

The wizard raised his hand and pointed northward, and with that she was forced to content herself. But she left the cave sadly enough to start on her second journey. On and on she went, till her body grew faint and her feet grew weary, but still her heart was brave. She could hardly have found her way, however, if all the birds and plants and insects had not joined to help her. Stella found that though she had no more power to make spells, yet she still understood the language of all living creatures. And it seemed as if they knew what her errand was, for the bushes bent out of her way, and the butterflies fanned her with their wings, and the birds hopped in front to show her the road.

"How is it that you are so good to me?" said Stella. "Perhaps the angels have told you to help me?"

And the branches rattled and the birds twittered, and the lark sprang high above her head, and sang a beautiful song about angels and the glorious place they dwell in.

At last they came to the willow bank, where sat the old witch under the roots of a dead willow, muttering to herself, and twisting the rotten twigs in her fingers.

"Oh, Witch of the Willow-bank," said Stella, "my brother is taken captive by the Black Dog. Tell me the way to go to him and how to fight with him, that I may set my brother free."

"What do you want to set him free for?" said the witch. "You think he will be grateful to you, but he won't. He will hate you because he owes you his life, for that is the way with bad hearts."

"I do not want him to be grateful," said Stella. "I only want to save him. Tell me how I may do it."

At last the witch said, "What will you give me if I do?"

"Alas!" said Stella, "I have nothing left to give."

"I am nearly blind," said the witch. "Give me your eyes, and I will tell you."

"That I cannot," replied Stella, "for how should I save my brother if I could not see? But I will give you one eye if you will tell me all you know, and help me all you can."

"Well, then, give it here, and I will," said the witch.

But Stella was too wise now for that.

"You shall tell me what to do first," she said. And after much persuading, the witch began:

"You must cross the swamp yonder until you reach an island on which is a cave; there lives the Black Dog. But do not go to the cave. Wait till the stars come out, and among them you will see a very bright one that changes to all manner of colours, red and blue, and green and yellow. That is Sirius, the dog-star. You must spread out your hands to it, and if your heart be pure and your desire firm, a spear will fall at your feet from the star; that is the only weapon that can slay the dog. But if your heart fail you, or your wishes be set on aught else than your brother's deliverance, you may spread your hands in vain, and the dog will kill you,—helpless as you are. Give me the eye you promised me."

"Here it is," said Stella. "But tell me, is there any particular part that I should aim at if I do come to fight the dog?"

"There is only one spot where he can be hurt."

"And where is it?"

"I will not tell you," said the witch. "You would not give me all I asked, so I will not tell you all you want. Go; you will get no more."

And Stella went sadly on her way; but still her courage did not fail. "If I am doing right," she said to herself, "perhaps the Lord of the angels will send and help me." So she journeyed on, and the land spread black before her, until towards evening she came to the borders of the swamp. Travelling became a difficult matter here; and as she picked her way slowly on she heard a sound behind her that made her cheek grow pale. It was the howling of wolves; she could see them in the gloomy twilight, dark figures gathering fast and following on her track. She plunged into the swamp and waded on, deep in the muddy waters; but the wolves gained upon her at every step. Nearer and nearer they came; she had given herself up for lost, when a hand caught hers, and a voice cried:

"Courage, Bo-peep! spring up here; we will baulk the rascals this time!"

The bog rang hard under her feet as she obeyed; and as her companion's breath smoked like vapour before them, she saw the water curdle and freeze wherever it spread. She found the ice firm enough to bear her light footsteps as they sped swiftly along; but it cracked and broke beneath the wolves, and soon they were left snarling and floundering far behind.

Now, Stella had time to wonder at her strange companion. He was all in white ; white plumes, that seemed a mixture of feather and palm-leaf and fern, floated from his head, and his dress was spangled all over with shapes of crystal, and moss and spar.

"Do you not know me?" he said, as Stella began to stammer her thanks. "Jack Frost is the name people give me. Why, you have often admired my handiwork on the banks and hedges."

"But I never met you before," said Stella. "Where should I have been if you had not come to my help to-night? If ever I can do anything——"

"Tut, tut," said Frost, "I have done nothing wonderful after all ; but if you want to do me a kindness, I will ask you to give me a smile whenever you see me. You are safe now, so I will be off to give the north wind a hint as to driving away those clouds, for I know you will want to see the stars." And he darted away without waiting for further thanks.

By the time that Stella had reached the island, the stars were shining brilliantly, and she had no difficulty in singling out Sirius, the many-changing dog-star. With mingled fear and hope she stretched her hands towards it, and lo, at her feet fell a spear, shining and many-coloured like the star from which it came! After a grateful upward glance she grasped her weapon and walked boldly round to the front of the cave. A large fire was burning at the mouth of it, beside which lay the huge mis-shapen Black Dog. Cosmo was passing to and fro with wood, which he piled on the fire, and it struck her to the heart to see how his likeness to the Black Dog was already growing. But she had not much time to look round her, for the dog rose up with bristling back and blood-shot eyes, and Cosmo fled to the back of the cave, while the dog sprang at Stella with a horrid growl. It was a strange battle and a fierce one. For a long time Stella could do no more than defend herself against him, for the spear, sharp though it was, rang harmless against the dog's thick hide. She felt her strength failing her, and gathering herself up for a last stroke, she thrust the spear down his open throat, and the dog leapt up, rolled over, and was dead.

Stella drew breath with a long sigh of relief, and went to seek out Cosmo as he sat cowering in the shadow. At first he seemed spell-bound or stupefied, though she spoke to him tenderly, calling him by the pet names of their childhood. At last he bowed his head and relieved himself by a fit of weeping. He told Stella all he had done, how he had gone from bad to worse, what evil thoughts he had nourished in his heart, and begged her to forgive him his ill-treatment of her. And when he raised his head, all trace of likeness to the Black Dog had vanished.

Now that her work was over, Stella turned very pale, and when Cosmo saw it, he laid her down gently and tended her as best he could, bidding her recover quickly, that they might go home together.

"Dear Cosmo, I think you will have to go without me," said Stella. "I am very weary, and a great longing has come over me to go up and be among the stars where you know the angels dwell. But promise me that you will not live alone. Go to the old woman who spent that night with me, and beg her to come and keep your house until you find another friend." Then she told him all she had learnt about the angels and the Lord of the angels, and how He saw all that people did, and besought her brother to be kind henceforth to all creatures, and to every one.

And Cosmo promised, listening with a full heart.

Before the morning dawn had made the stars grow pale, an angel stooped to beckon her, and Stella mounted up to join the starry host.

"It is well," said Cosmo, as he watched her upward flight. "I did not deserve to keep her, and she is far happier there." And as he gazed a small new star shone out in the sky beside Sirius, and Cosmo knew that it was his sister.

The sun had risen when Cosmo crossed the swamp, so that he did not encounter the wolves, but he soon found himself wandering, doubtful of the way, for all the birds and insects shrank away at his approach, remembering how he had been wont to treat them. Then Cosmo made a mournful little song, and sang it as he went along :

> " I have a little sister, they call her Bo-peep,
> She wades through the waters, deep, deep ;
> She climbs through the heavens, high, high :
> Poor little sister,—she has but one eye !"

When the creatures round heard this song they said : " This is Bo-peep's brother, whom she went to save : come, let us help him for her sake." And the birds flew circling round him, and the grasshoppers hopped in front to show him the path, and the flowers looked up at him and smiled. And still, when he saw that little star twinkling above him, or its reflection quivering in some pool at his feet, he sang his song as he journeyed on. So he reached the cottage in the wold at last.

The old woman came to live with him when he asked her, as Stella had begged him to do. Her neighbours said she would repent it, but she never did, for Cosmo was quite changed now. And before long the cottage in the wold, instead of being shunned and feared, became the resort of all that were in trouble, whether man or beast. For Cosmo henceforth used his magical powers to heal instead of to hurt, and his name became known throughout the country as the friend of those that were in need.

Every starry night Cosmo went out to greet Stella, his star that had done so much for him, and Stella smiled down on him again. She is still shining there ; and her smile is always brightest when Frost is at work on earth below. She has learnt the language of the angels now.

PUSSYCAT AT COURT.

II.—PUSSYCAT.

ONCE upon a time there lived in the south of England a poor man who ought to have been a very rich man, for he was heir to the great estate of Wealthydale. But when the old Lord of Wealthydale died, some distant cousins of his said that his will was not a good one, and that they ought to have his property. They went to law about it, and they spent all their money, and the rightful heir spent all his money, and still it was never settled who should have it. So the fields were not sown, and the cattle were not tended, and Wealthydale Castle fell to ruin, while its real owner lived in a little tumble-down cottage outside the park gates.

He had no money left to pay wages, so his servants went away from him one after the other, until there was only one creature left in the house with him, and that was the cat. She was a very handsome cat, and came of a good family too, for she was the great-great-great-great-grandchild of Puss-in-Boots. She often wished that her great-great-great-great-grandfather's boots had not been worn out long before her time, for she was very fond of her master, and wished she could do something to help him.

"Why do you stay with me, Pussycat?" said her master. That was her name, for she had always been called Pussycat. "I have no cows now, and I cannot afford to buy you milk."

"Do you think I am such a bad mouser that I cannot catch mice enough to feed me?" replied Pussycat. "You need not think I am going away, master. Why, what would become of your cheese and candles, if I were not here to look after them?"

"Well, you are a good little Pussycat," said her master, "and as soon as I have brought out my discovery you shall have everything that you can want."

Pussycat turned away her head that he might not see her smile, for the great discovery that her master was going to make was, what glowworms' light is made of. As soon as he had found this out, he meant to invent lamps that should be lighted in the same way, and felt sure that he should make his fortune by them; but Pussycat did not feel sure. Her master spent all his time in trying to make this discovery, except that he worked a little in his garden; but meantime the money was all spent, and the cottage roof was falling in, and things looked worse and worse. Even pussy was hard up, for she had destroyed all the rats and mice of the neighbourhocd.

"Dear master," she said one day, "how soon will you invent your glowworm light? for we are sadly in want of a few shillings."

"Well, Pussycat," he said, "I begin to be afraid that I shall not succeed for some time, unless I could get a firefly to compare with them. I could easily send for some if I only had my estate, but they are not to be had any nearer than Italy, and it would cost too much."

"I'll tell you what, master," said Pussycat, sitting very upright. "You go to London and speak to the King, and get him to make a law that you are to have your estate back again."

"The King is so busy, I am afraid he would not listen to me, Pussycat."

"Speak to the Queen, then."

"I am afraid that would not do any better, Pussycat."

"Well, if my master won't go, I will," thought Pussycat. "I know I am only a poor little puss, but my master has been very good to me, and what a pleasant thing it would be if I could do him some good in return."

But Pussycat was afraid to tell what she meant to do, lest her master should say it would be of no use. So she only said, "Master, will you give me a holiday for a few days ? I want to go away on a visit."

"Certainly, my good Pussycat," he replied. "But you must have some money for your journey : here is all I have got, take as much as you like."

"Well, it is no bad thing to have a little money in one's pocket," observed Pussycat, thinking that the money would be well spent if it got back the estate. She counted it, and found that there was five-pence halfpenny. "This will be plenty," said she, taking the halfpenny. She wrapped it in a beech-leaf, tucked it carefully under her left fore-leg, and very early the next morning she began her journey to London.

It so happened that at that time the King was gone on a visit to Wales, and only the Queen remained at home in the great London palace. She was sitting on her chair of state, embroidering a pair of gloves, as a present for the King when he came back, and her ladies were sitting working and talking round her, when suddenly one of them stopped and said, "Hark! I fancied I heard a noise."

Scrabble scrabble scrabble, it went ; scratch scratch scratch.

"Dear me, what can it be ?" said the Queen, jumping up.

"Oh !" cried one of the ladies, and fainted away on the spot, while all the others screamed and ran about. But they could not find out where it was, nor what it was.

"Perhaps it was your Majesty's little dog Joujou," suggested one of the ladies.

"No," said the Queen, "for I have sent Joujou out to take a walk with the youngest page. Perhaps it was nothing at all, and anyhow here comes our luncheon, so let us sit down and eat it."

But scarcely had they sat down when—Scrabble scrabble scrabble, scratch scratch scratch !

"Oh, there it is again !" cried the Queen. And she dropped the spoonful of whipped cream and honey that she was going to eat, all down her lap, and ran out into the middle of the room. All her ladies ran out too, and there they stood, looking about them.

" It sounded just under her Majesty's chair," said one of the ladies presently, in a whisper.

"So it did," said the Queen. · " Lady Alice, go and look underneath, and see if you can find anything there."

" I really—I should be very happy," said Lady Alice, "only stooping always makes my head ache. Suppose you go and look, Lady Bertha."

"Oh no, indeed I cannot," said Lady Bertha. "I should be frightened out of my wits for fear something should jump out at me."

"Scrabble scrabble scrabble, scratch scratch scratch !" replied the thing under the chair. At the same moment a page opened the door and said, " Please your Majesty—he he he he he !"

"Stop laughing, you unmannerly boy !" commanded the Queen, " and say what you have got to say."

"Will your Majesty please to grant an audience to—he he he he he !" replied the page.

"Certainly," said the Queen. "It is the Spanish ambassador, no doubt. Behave properly, you naughty boy, and show him in."

And the Queen put herself into a stately attitude, and her ladies grouped themselves behind her, and the page threw open the door, and in marched—Pussycat. As soon as they saw her, the Queen and all her ladies clapped their hands together and laughed, even more than the page had done. It was not much wonder that they laughed so ; for Pussycat, wishing to show her respect for the Queen, had spent her halfpenny in half a yard of blue ribbon, which she had tied round her neck, leaving two long ends. And as she was told that ladies always wore feathers to go to Court, she had picked up in the fields a tall black feather out of a rook's wing, and had stuck it upright on the top of her head, so that it went wiggle-waggle at every step. Pussycat was not a bit taken aback at being received like this, for she thought it might be the Royal way of welcoming a guest. So she walked straight up to the Queen, and stretched herself and gave a great yawn, which is the height of cat-civility.

"Oh, what a nice little cat! Here, puss, puss, puss!" said the Queen, throwing down a reel of coloured silk for her to play with. Pussycat just gave it a tap for politeness' sake; but she thought the Queen might have known that she was not a kitten. Just as the Queen was going to roll it again, the ladies began to scream, for there was the noise—scrabble scrabble scrabble, scratch scratch scratch—louder than ever.

Now Pussycat, who had hunted mice all her life, knew at once that it was nothing but a little mouse under the chair, and in a moment she was there herself. When the poor little mouse saw this great creature come bouncing in, with ribbons fluttering, and feather wagging, and whiskers bristling, he was in such a fright that he cried—

"Squeak, squeak! Oh, please don't hurt me—squeak! and I will run away and never come back again. Squeak, squeak!"

And away he scuttled as fast as ever his terrified legs could go. Pussycat came out from under the chair again, with her tail very upright.

"Oh, the good cat ! Oh, the excellent pussy ! She has frightened it quite away," cried all the ladies.

"You shall stay with me and be my pussy," said the Queen, stroking her.

But Pussycat jerked her tail from side to side, which is the same among cats as shaking one's head ; and she answered, "I would not stay, not if your Majesty should give me two cows for myself, and the key of the royal larder."

"Why not ?" said the Queen.

"Because I could not bear to leave my master ?" replied Pussycat.

"And who is your master, little puss ?" said the Queen.

Then Pussycat told her all about her master and his estate, and why she had come to London. And the Queen listened, and said she would do what she could. Only she begged Pussycat not to tell anybody a word about it, for she should like it to be a surprise to him.

Pussycat rubbed herself against the leg of the Queen's chair, and promised to keep it a secret. Then, for joy at having succeeded so well in her errand, she ran round after her tail, caught it, pretended to kill it vigorously with her hind paws, and then gave three jumps with her legs stuck out very stiff, and scampered out of the palace. She lost no time in the journey home again, and when she reached the cottage she found her master sitting studying glowworm light as usual. He looked up when she came in, and said—

" Pussycat, Pussycat, where have you been ?"
" I've been to London, to see the Queen,"

replied Pussycat. Her master said again—

> " Pussycat, Pussycat, what did you there ?"
> " I frightened a little mouse under a chair."

"Ah, well," said her master, "I am glad you have come safe home again. You did not see any glowworms as you came along, did you? I am particularly in want of one just now."

Before long, Pussycat met the neighbours. They all knew that she had been away from home, and every one asked the same question—

> " Pussycat, Pussycat, where have you been ?"

And Pussycat always replied—

> " I've been to London, to see the Queen !"
> " Pussycat, Pussycat, what did you there ?"
> " I frightened a little mouse under a chair."

And some of them would add—

> " Pussycat, Pussycat, what did you more ?"
> " I came back the same way I went by before."
> " But, Pussycat, Pussycat, what did you bring ?"
> " A feather that fell from some passing rook's wing."

"Well, then," they would say, "it certainly was not worth while to go."

But then Pussycat would wink knowingly to herself, and think that it certainly had been quite worth while. Not a word did she say, however, not even when five hundred workmen came down from London and began to rebuild and furnish Wealthydale Castle, so as to make it better than it had ever been before. Pussycat went up every day to inspect the work ; and by-and-by she found tailors, and hatters, and hosiers there, inquiring for the master of Wealthydale.

"He is staying in one of his cottages while his castle is being repaired," said Pussycat. "But you must not mind if he should tell you that he is not the owner of Wealthydale, for he takes strange fancies sometimes. And if he says anything about glowworms, you may be sure that he is the right person."

The tradespeople thanked her and went to find the cottage. The first person who knocked at the door was the tailor, and he asked—

"Is the lord of Wealthydale at home ?"

"There are no lords here," replied Pussycat's master. "I am only a poor glowworm-hunter."

"Oh, it's all right then," said the tailor, and at once began to take his measure. Round his arm, round his shoulders, round his waist, flew the active bit of tape.

"Dear me, dear me !" said Pussy's master, "this poor man must be out of his mind. I must keep very quiet, for fear he should do something violent."

So he stood quite still until the tailor had finished, and then gave a great sigh of relief. But no sooner was he gone than up came the shoemaker with the same inquiry.

"If you are looking for lords, you had better go to the Castle," replied Pussycat's master. "No one lives here except a poor student of glowworms' light."

"Oh, very good, I understand," said the shoemaker, and

out he whipped his foot-rule, and down he went on his knees to measure the student's foot.

"Dear, dear, dear, this is another of them!" said the poor man. "How very unfortunate! I wonder what he is going to do to my foot?"

After the shoemaker came the hosier, and the hatter, and the glover. When Pussycat came in to dinner, her master said—

"I am afraid they must have built a madhouse near us, Pussycat. I have had such a number of madmen here this morning."

"Indeed!" said Pussycat. "If they come again I will go and speak to the Inspector of Nuisances." And she set to work washing her face, to hide a smile.

Before long, the new things came home. Pussycat stole up when her master was in bed, and taking away all his old clothes, she hung the new ones in their place. When her master got up he was thinking so hard, as usual, of glowworms, that he never noticed the change until on putting on his coat he missed the hole in which he always caught his little finger. "Halloo, is this my coat?" he said. "And where is that patch on my right knee gone to? and the crack in my boot? Pussycat! do you see anything strange in my looks this morning?"

"No, master," said Pussycat, trying to keep her whiskers steady; "you look all right to me."

"Well, I suppose it was my fancy, then." And her master sat down to his work as usual.

In the afternoon Pussycat proposed a walk, and led the way through the park towards the castle. When they came in sight of it her master said, "Why I do believe somebody has been repairing the house!"

"Let us go in and see it," said Pussycat, and in they went. The servants all came to meet him, and went about asking his opinion of this thing, and what he would like done with that thing; and the more he told them that he was not the master of the place at all, but only a hunter for glowworms, the more they bowed, and smiled, and nodded to one another. They were still in the house when there was a noise of clattering of horse-hoofs and rumbling of wheels.

"There is somebody coming," said Pussycat. "Let us go and see who it is." And when they came to the hall door, behold it was the Queen herself, with all her ladies, and pages, and attendants. Nobody else came forward to open the carriage door, so Pussycat's master did it.

As the Queen entered the hall she said, "I am glad to be the first to wish the master of Wealthydale joy on his return to his own house."

"Please your Majesty, I am not the master of Wealthydale," replied he. "I have been telling everybody so all day, only they will not believe me."

"Yes, but you are," said the Queen. "Your estate is given back to you by law, for Pussycat came and told me all about it, and I have had matters set right. I hope you will be very happy here, and do a great deal of good in the neighbourhood."

"Dear me, is all Wealthydale mine?" he exclaimed. "What a great deal I shall have to do! However, Pussycat, now I shall be able to send to Italy for some fireflies."

"As for you, little Puss," said the Queen, "you have kept my secret so well that I make you a lady in your own right, and you shall have a place at court whenever you will come and visit us."

Pussycat rubbed her cheek against the Queen's hand, and gently bit her finger, to show her gratitude. She never went to court again herself, however, for she found plenty to do in the castle. But she was married soon afterwards to a very gentlemanly cat, who undertook to look after the stables and granaries, and as soon as her eldest daughter was of age to come out, she sent her to court, where she became a great favourite.

The master of Wealthydale became so busy before long in attending to his farm, and his people, and his schools, that the secret of the glowworms' light remains undiscovered to this day.

Pussycat had a large and prosperous family. Even now you may know her descendants by a mark like a coronet which they wear stamped on their foreheads. Her great delight was to sit by the fire in her master's library, and to tell her grandchildren the wonderful story of how she had been on a journey to London to visit the Queen; how she was dressed up, and what she did there; and how frightened poor Mousey was under the chair.

JACK AND GILL AT THE ENCHANTED WELL.

III.—JACK AND GILL.

ONCE upon a time a brother and sister named Jack and Gill lived in a little cottage in a pleasant wooded valley. They were young, very young, the neighbours said, to set up house all alone ; but they had no one belonging to them, and as they were hardworking, healthy children, they got on very well. Jack dug in the garden and fished in the stream, and gained many a loaf of bread and piece of meat by cutting firewood in the forest for the farmers and cottagers round. Gillian washed and baked and kept their home tidy, and when her other work was done she would sit and spin the flax which her brother planted in their little strip of field. The Baron, whose great grey stone castle stood on the hill above, was very kind to them, and only charged them half the rent for their cottage that he might otherwise have had ; and at Christmas he always sent them a present, a new cloak for Gillian or a jerkin for Jack. He was so kind to all his tenants that there was great mourning when the old Baron died, and the barony passed into other hands.

The new Baron was a stranger, and even a foreigner, people said, for he and his household spoke among themselves in a foreign tongue. He was stiff and cold and silent, very different to the kindly old Baron ; and the people, who had made up their minds to dislike him before he came, soon began to hate him. He had new ways of farming which they did not like, and they grumbled even at his improvements. Jack and Gill grumbled too ; for the new Baron did not spare them like the old, but charged them their full rent, and Jack and Gill felt themselves very hardly used.

"What did we want with a stranger like that coming to set himself over us ?" growled Jack. "We'll show him that we are as good as he, for all his pride. Our good old ways won't do for him, indeed, and we must alter them all to please him !"

" He does not seem to get much pleasure out of that or anything else," said Gill. " I had rather live here in our little cottage, although there is a hole in the roof, than up there in his great gloomy castle."

There was one person in his great gloomy castle, however, whom the Baron loved so dearly that she was like a gleam of sunshine to him, and that was his little daughter. When she rode out beside him on her pony, the country people noticed that the grave Baron could smile and talk with his bright little girl ; and he was always finding out some present or some new excursion to give her pleasure. After a time the little Lady Edda was no longer to be met in the lanes and on the heath; and when the Baron came out, which was not often, he looked more dark and stern than ever. And one day Jack brought home the news that the Baron's little girl was very ill. He sent far and wide for doctors to come and cure her; and they came, but they could none of them do her any good. At last the Baron sent for an old doctor who had been born in the place, and he said, "Nothing will cure her except it be a bath from the waters of the enchanted well on the top of the opposite hill."

"Let one of my yeomen go at once and fill a pitcher at that well," commanded the Baron.

So the man went. But as he came down the hill again with his full pitcher, his foot slipped, the pitcher was broken, and all the water spilt.

The Baron chid him for his carelessness, without heeding his excuse that the ground itself had seemed to give way beneath him, and sent another of his servants up to the enchanted well. But his pitcherful met with the same fate. Yet another and another went, and the Baron grew angry and fierce, for not one of them but fell and spilled his water before he reached the foot of the hill. The villagers gathered together to watch them, and laughed as one after another came tumbling down with his load.

"Why is it that they cannot bring the water safely to the bottom of the hill?" asked Gillian.

"Because they are all strangers and intruders," replied a

man among the crowd ; and the well, be it enchanted or not,
is a good English well, and likes them no better than we do."

"Enchanted ? of course it is," said a very old woman, who
was commonly called Granny Bridget. "Why, neighbour
Thorlson, my grandmother used to say she could mind the
time when that well was a merry streamlet flowing all down
this valley. But it came in the way of a wizard who lived on
the hillside under the old ash-tree stump yonder, and he laid
a spell on it, and there it lies imprisoned in its cave until such
time as its waters may be drawn and put to some good and
noble use. But no one has ever yet loosed the spell."

"If strangers cannot do it," said Gill, "why do not some
of our own people go up and try what can be done ?"

"And serve the Baron ? not I !" said Thorlson. "If he
wants our help, let him come himself and ask us for it. He
has been proud and haughty enough, let him be a bit humbled
now. There goes another of them, soiling his fine coat !"

Gillian did not like to watch any longer, and went back into
her cottage. She busied herself there for some time, when a
louder talking than usual made her look out again, and she
saw the Baron himself coming slowly and carefully down the
hill, carrying a pitcher of water. But even as she looked, he
too slipped and fell like all the rest. And when the people
saw it they laughed ; but Jack felt too sorry for the poor
father to laugh. The Baron did not seem to care for their
laughter ; he got up and shook the dust from his cloak, and
pulling his cap lower over his eyes, passed through the crowd
as if he did not observe that there was any one there.

"He don't care a bit," said one of the men.

"He does, though," said Jack. And while the others went to watch the Baron as he strode home, Jack turned to look at the precious pitcherful of water that was trickling uselessly down the path. As he looked, he saw a little thin mist, like steam, rising from the spilt water, and a sound came from it, though so faint that he could hardly feel sure that he heard it, which seemed to say—

> " Jack and Gill,
>   Go up the hill,
> And fetch a pail of water.
>   Jack and Gill,
>   Give good for ill,
> And save the stranger's daughter."

"Why, who said that ?" exclaimed Jack.

"Yes, Jack, do let us," cried Gill.

"Let us what ?"

"Why, give good for ill, and save the stranger's daughter."

"What, you heard it too ?" said Jack. "Then it could not have been fancy. But I don't see what we have got to do with it, and you know the Baron has raised our rent, and he is so proud that he will hardly say 'Good morning,' if a fellow takes off his cap to him."

"But the little girl," said Gillian. "And it would be doing good, you know."

"But the Baron is rich, and he ought to do good to us," objected Jack.

"So he ought," said Gill ; "but that dosen't make any difference in our duty to him, does it ? Why, he is just as much our neighbour as old Bridget, whose pigsty you worked at so hard yesterday."

Jack pushed his cap on to the back of his head, and looked puzzled. "H'm, I suppose he is, though I can't say I ever thought much about it. I shouldn't wonder but you are in the right, Gill. Anyhow, if you will go up and fetch a pail of water to-morrow morning, I'll go with you."

Very early the next morning, before the sun had risen, Jack and Gill were on their way up the hill, and soon reached the enchanted well. The water looked very dark and mysterious in its deep rocky cave. A few blackened fronds of hartstongue fern trailed over the mouth, and there was a tinkling echo within as of drops of water falling into the pool. But Jack and Gill stayed neither to look nor to listen. Hastily drawing the water, they began their journey down again, carrying the pail between them.

"Steadily, Gill," said Jack; "don't slip, or you will be down."

"I cannot help it," said Gill; "it feels to me as if the whole hill were shaking. And what is that strange rumbling noise that I hear behind me?"

"It must be a storm coming up behind the hill," answered Jack; "yet it looked fine enough when we started. Never mind, Gill; we are more than half way down now. Ha, ha! they will find that we can do what all the fine serving-lads and men-at-arms—holloa!" For before Jack could finish his speech down he fell, and over he rolled, cutting his forehead pretty sharply upon a stone in the way. Down went the pail, and out poured all the water, and Gill came tumbling after upon the top of all.

"Oh, what a pity!" she said, looking at the empty pail. "But, dear Jack, you have hurt yourself; is it very bad?" And she dipped her kerchief in the slop, and began to bathe his forehead.

"That does me good; I hardly feel it now," said Jack. "O, sister, look!" He pointed to the enchanted water, for lo! the same white mist that they had seen before was rising from it, and they were now so near that they could see that it took the form of a beautiful maiden. Every fold in her robe was distinct, and yet she was so transparent that they saw plainly the woods and sky behind her. Her robe sparkled in the rays of the rising sun, like myriads of dewdrops, and the same musical voice seemed to float towards them from her:

> " Think upon the Baron's need,
>   Try again the kindly deed,
>   And save his little daughter.
>   Lesser haste makes better speed,
>   Jack and Gill,
>   Go up the hill,
>   And fetch a pail of water."

"I know they say, 'More haste worst speed,'" said Jack to himself; "but I suppose the other is the fairy way of putting it."

And Gillian whispered, "O, Jack, how beautiful! Do let us go again, as she says."

"And tumble down and break my head again," said Jack. "Never mind, it will be worth while, if it cures the little girl; so come along, Gill."

They were soon beside the enchanted well again.   Instead of dipping their pail at once, they remembered the dew-drop maiden's warning, and stopped this time to look and to listen. And as they stood, the tinkling echo within the cave seemed to form itself into words, and said—

> " Take a pebble from the brink,
>   Let it in the waters sink ;
>   Pluck a daisy from the brim,
>   Let it on the waters swim ;
>   Three times thirty count the charm :
>   Dip and fill, and fear not harm."

" That will not be very hard to do," said Gill.   Only can you count up to thirty, Jack ?"

" Thirty !   Yes, or a hundred," said Jack ; "and more too. Only I am not quite sure about the millions and billions."

" Well, luckily, we shan't want them," replied Gill.

Then Jack took up a white pebble that touched the very brink of the water, and dropped it in.   And Gillian plucked a daisy, whose white leaflets kissed the water's brim, and flung it in.   Immediately the well began to toss and foam, and bubble and boil, until it seemed as if the cave could not hold it all ; and the hill rumbled and shook as it had done when they had fallen down.

Gillian was frightened, and held fast by her brother.   But Jack put his arm round her, and boldly began to count.   And when he had counted the first thirty, the shaking of the hill ceased.   When he had counted the second thirty, the well left off tossing its spray over the ferns and mosses.   And by the time he had counted the third thirty, it was as calm, and smooth, and still, as if nothing had ever ruffled it, not even a dragon-fly's wing. The pebble shone white at the bottom, and the daisy floated motionless on the top. And the children dipped and filled without fear, and went safely and joyously down the hill, and up again on the other side of the valley, until they stood before the castle gate. The warder was standing there armed from head to foot, as though he were every moment expecting an enemy to arrive. He let the children go in, however, as soon as he saw the pail of water, and called to a gaily-dressed squire to lead them to the hall. Here the Baron himself met them. Now Jack had made a fine speech as they came along, which he was to say to the Baron when he gave him the pail ; but behold, when the time came, the speech was all gone, and he could think of nothing better to say than,

" Please, sir, here's the water you wanted."

" I will gladly take it, my lad, if it be really from the right well," replied the Baron.

Jack did not know that somebody had been trying to get money from him the day before by bringing him water that was not drawn from the enchanted well, and he answered in a huff—

" Oh, if you doubt our word, you need not take it : it doesn't matter to us."

" Oh, but do, sir !" said Gillian. "We brought it because the doctor said it would do the little Lady Edda good."

The Baron looked at them for a moment, and then suddenly took up the pail and went away with it. The squire went after, offering to carry it for the Baron, and Jack and Gill were left alone in the hall.

They waited and waited, but the Baron did not come back, nor send them any message. They grew very tired, but they dared not sit down, lest the Baron should come in. They were hungry, too, for they had not breakfasted. At last Gillian, speaking in a very low voice — for she was a little frightened in that great hall—ventured to say, “ Jack, do you think they have forgotten us ?”

“ I am sure they have,” said Jack. “ Come along, we’ll go home.”

“ I should like to know about the little girl,” said Gill, lingering. But Jack took her hand and said—

“ You will know soon enough—come on. I want my breakfast, don’t you ?”

But when the day passed away and evening came, and there had been no message from the castle, Jack grew very indignant, and said it was a shame of the Baron ; he might have said “ Thank you ” for the trouble they had taken, at the very least.

“ And sent us back our pail,” added Gill. “ But I dare say he is with his little daughter.”

“ Catch me doing anything for him again, that’s all,” said Jack. “ I am glad the neighbours don’t know that we went to fetch the pail of water.”

The next day at noon, however, just as Jack and Gill were finishing dinner, in walked the gaily-dressed squire with the pail in his hand.

"My lord the Baron returns you this with many thanks," he said. "And he desires your presence immediately at the castle."

Jack looked as if he had no mind to go, but Gill cried, "Wait a moment for me, Jack, and I shall be ready to come with you." And with that she ran and fetched him his Sunday jerkin, for indeed his week-day one was nothing but patches and darns.

So they started in company with the squire. Gillian's first question was, "How is the little Lady Edda? did the water do her good?"

"Good!" said the squire. "It put fresh life in her at once. "Why, we thought she was dying fast: my master was like one distraught."

"What was the matter with her," asked Jack.

"She seemed to be pining away," answered the squire, "partly for want of companions, and partly for love of her native land."

"She was born in another country, then?"

"Yes," said the squire, "in beautiful Normandy. Why, for the matter of that, we are all strangers here; and the trouble we have had to learn your tongue! My lord the Baron is only just beginning to speak it rightly now."

"That was what made him so slow to answer, then, when we greeted him!" exclaimed Jack. "But what made him leave his own land, if he loved it so well?"

"Troubles and misfortunes," said the squire. He has had plenty of them; but I do not see that we are any better off here, for there is no one to cheer him with a friendly word."

Did barons want cheering? It seemed odd; nevertheless Jack made up his mind to speak more civilly to him if he had a chance. The chance soon came, for the Baron met them again in the hall, and thanked them so heartily for what they had done for his child, that Jack made bold to ask after her.

"Come and see her yourselves," said the Baron. "She is wishing to thank you also." And he led the way up flights of stairs, and along galleries and passages, till Jack began to wonder how many men it would take to defend the castle against an enemy, and Gill thought what work it must be to sweep it all out every day. At last the Baron stopped and opened a door, and they followed him into a room—but what a room it was! Jack and Gill had never even imagined anything so grand. There were Persian carpets on the floor, and silken tapestry on the walls, and painted glass in the windows, and on a carved couch in the middle of the room there lay a pretty little pale fair-haired girl. There were pictures, and toys, and rare shells strewed about her; but she did not seem to care for them, or even to notice them. She looked up as they entered, and when she saw Jack and Gill's faces of wonder and admiration, she suddenly clapped her hands together and laughed merrily. The Baron looked quite pleased, and said, "Go to the Lady Edda, children."

Gill made a step forward, but Jack was seized with such a fit of shyness that he would not stir until the little girl came and led them in.   She showed them her treasures, which were all new and wonderful to Jack and Gill, and told them about the pictures, and made them listen to the sound of ocean waves that still lingers in the hollow shells, and grew quite eager and delighted at their delight. The time went so fast, that when Jack at last looked up, he was dismayed to see how near sunset it was, and said that they must go home at once. Then little Edda pulled her father's head down close to her, and whispered something to him ; and the Baron said to Jack and Gill, " My little girl is lonely here with no one to play with ; if you will come and spend at any rate the greater part of your days with her, I will feed and clothe and take care of you."

Jack and Gill hardly knew what to answer, but the Baron saw that they would like it, and he said, " You, Gillian, shall be my daughter's companion and attendant ; and you, Jack, shall be her page, and accompany her in her walks, and lead her horse when she rides."

" Oh, I'm sure !" said Jack, and then he could not think what more to say ; so he and Gill bowed and curtsied with all their might, and little Edda called out to them as they went away to mind and come early to-morrow.

The neighbours had heard of their visit to the castle, and were waiting at Jack and Gill's cottage to question them about it. They had so muc to tell about the Baron's kindness, and what the squire had told them about his troubles, and how he was only just learning to speak the language, that even neighbour Thorlson began to think that his shy, silent manner might not be all from pride and sulkiness. So next time that the Baron rode into the valley, instead of glum looks and faces turned away, he met with civil greetings, to which he answered so readily, that before long the Baron and his people were great friends, and they even began to allow that there might be some sense in his new plans and ways of farming.

As for Jack and Gill, they spent almost all their time at the castle. Little Edda grew better so fast that in a few days she was able to go out on her pony, with Jack holding the bridle, and Gill walking by her side.

"Let us go to the glen where the dry watercourse is," said Gill; "it is so pretty there." And they threaded their way to it among the bushes.

Presently Jack said, "I fancy I can hear a sound of running water, as if the dry bed had a stream in it again. Yes, it has, too; and yet we have had no heavy rain. Why, Gill!" he exclaimed, after looking about him, "this stream must come from the enchanted well!"

"Then the spell is broken and its waters are free again! I am so glad!" said Gillian. And she and Jack told Edda all the story of how they had gone up the hill to fetch a pail of water, and how Jack tumbled down, and about the dewdrop maiden, and what old Bridget had told them about the well.

"I am very glad you went to fetch the water," said Edda, "and did as the dewdrop maiden told you. How beautiful she must be! I do so wish I could see her."

"Look, yonder, where the stream falls over the rocks," said Jack. "I thought I saw the wave of her mantle then, as the sunbeam slanted across the spot."

Edda slid down from her pony, and the three children went to the edge of the little waterfall, and stood gazing in delight at the beautiful dewdrop maiden who was there, hovering in her rainbow robe amid the spray.

"Hark," said Gillian, presently; "I think I can hear the same sweet tinkling song that we heard before."

Yes, the stream was singing as it bounded joyously from stone to stone, and this was the song that the children heard :

> "Joy, joy, for my wave
> Is no more a slave
> In the darksome cave;
> I am free, I am free!
> I may leap down the hills, I may glide o'er the lea,
> I may scatter fresh showers to grass and tree,
> I may join my stream-sisters who call to me,
> And with them embracing, so glad, so free,
> I may flow, I may go, to the far-away sea!"

"Are you going so far, bright stream?" said little Edda. "Then take this flower with you to the sea and bid him bear it to the shores of my fair Normandy, and carry this message with it, that we have found good friends and kind words and loving hearts, and we are happy now at last in our new English home."

And the dancing wavelets leaped up and caught the flower, and the stream sang more sweetly than ever as it bore it along, for the song it sang was of the power of kindliness and love.

IV.—HICKORY DICKORY DOCK.

" Hickory dickory dock,
The mouse ran up the clock ;
The clock struck one, the mouse ran down,
Hickory dickory dock."

ONCE upon a time there were three brother-mice named Hickory, Dickory, and Dock, who lived together behind a carved oak cabinet in the hall of a large, rambling house. Not far from them stood an old-fashioned cuckoo clock, and under it there lived a beautiful lady-mouse, named Glossyfur. Now all three of the brothers, Hickory, Dickory, and Dock, wanted to marry Glossyfur. And when they found that they could not make up their minds which of them should have her, they agreed to fight about it.

But it so happened that Glossyfur was just then taking a walk past the oak cabinet, and when she heard what Hickory, Dickory, and Dock were talking about, she called them to her and said—

"You must not fight, for it is very wrong and very silly. If you do, not one of you shall marry me."

"But we cannot agree about it," said the brothers.

"I will tell you how it shall be settled," said Glossyfur

HICKORY DICKORY DOCK.

Page 46.

"You know that the old clock under whom I live is a great friend of mine, and he has promised to give me a home inside his case when I marry. But he has been in very low spirits lately, because the last time that Master Tom came home from school he tied up the cuckoo with a needleful of sewing-cotton, so that she can neither sing nor clap her wings. This naturally annoys the clock very much ; and I propose that whichever of you will go up and bite away the cotton and set the cuckoo free, shall be my husband and live with me in the clock-case."

All three of the brothers said they were ready to do it.

"Then," said Glossyfur, "Hickory shall have the first turn, because he is the eldest."

"Oh, but that is not fair at all !" cried Dickory and Dock. "That gives us no chance, for it is so easy, he is sure to do it."

Glossyfur replied that they must either do her way or not at all.   The mice still grumbled, and how long the discussion might have gone on it is hard to say, if the clock himself had not interrupted it.

"Crrp ! Only two minutes to twelve," he said.   "Now is your time, if one of you means to come."

For you know the cuckoo only came out of her little house once every hour, just before the clock was going to strike.

Up ran Hickory as fast as he could, and as he got to the top of the clock, out came the cuckoo. Hickory saw the cotton that tied her plainly enough, and lost no time in beginning to gnaw it. But he had hardly begun, when there came a great

"Oh, stop! Oh, don't go in the dark!" cried the butler, who was really in a terrible fright by this time.

"Wait one moment—I am getting a light," said Edelherz. And he began splittering and spluttering at the matches, striking them at the wrong end, letting them go out again when they had lit, and altogether making such a fuss over it, that when at last they did sally forth, armed with candles and pokers, there was nobody to be fonnd anywhere. Thereupon they began quarrelling as to whether it had not been all fancy from beginning to end; and Edelherz took advantage of this second hubbub to disappear also.

The person who was probably in the greatest alarm of all during the uproar was the queen herself. She found King Siegfried awaiting her, wrapped in the velvet gown, having filed away and broken the bars of his prison so as to scramble through them.

They could whisper as low as they pleased, now that they were close together, and the queen told him how he was to peep out and see that there was nobody in the passage; and then when he heard a great scuffle in one of the rooms, to run quickly past, and not to stop until he reached the potato-loft.

"There Edelherz our page will join you," said the queen, "and you and he can settle how best to assemble our loyal subjects and regain the throne."

"But the next time that the sentinel summons me——" began the king.

"I shall answer," said Queen Holda.

"You! I cannot leave you in this prison. What if I should fail——"

"You will not fail," interrupted the queen. "That is, if you go at once. Quick, or all will have been in vain!"

Then Siegfried rushed away up the steps, and the queen remained alone in the darkness. She could hear a faint sound of running about and of voices overhead. Then it stopped. Had they caught him? had he escaped? How should she bear to wait there the whole night without knowing? She was getting so impatient that she felt as if she must go up and see, when a well-known voice sounded through the loop-hole—

> "Hark, hark! the dogs do bark,
> Beggars are coming to town;
> Some in rags——"

"Hold your tongue, and get away with you!" crid the sentinel angrily. But the queen was satisfied now. They had succeeded so far, then, and her faithful page had come to let her know it. But they had still to go and collect the nobles and leaders of the people, and then to fight; and Schurk had the whole army under his orders. Oh, when would it be morning? Surely, more than an hour must have passed. It was still some time, however, before the sentinel made his call, and when he did so the queen was so startled, although she had been expecting it every moment, that she could hardly get up voice enough to answer, "Here I am." The next time it was not so startling; but how slowly the night did pass! It seemed to Queen Holda like a week of nights all gathered into one. There was no sound of commotion in the town ; no footstep in the sleeping palace ; nothing to break the long silence except the hourly challenge of the sentinel.

At length the queen hailed the first glimmering of dawn through her narrow loophole slit, and almost before she could feel sure that day had really come, she was aware of a growing commotion in the city. There were distant shouts, and the trampling of hundreds of feet ; and then came a banging of doors and a rushing to and fro overhead. What had happened, or was going to happen ? Would Edelherz find time to signal to her again ? While the queen was listening, she heard the door above burst open, and steps came hastily towards her.

Madam—madam !" said the page's voice, "come out quickly. All the city has risen on our side—the king is in the palace yard—the scullery window is yet unguarded— haste, haste, and we shall join them !"

They reached the passage as he spoke ; but they were only just in time, for steps pursued them down, and as they dropped safely to the ground outside the scullery window, there was a crash of broken wine-bottles behind them, and the butler's voice exclaimed, " Two Edelherzes ! Oh, come and save me, somebody !" and the shutters were barred and bolted.

The queen had no time to think of her own strange appearance in the page's dress ; for the palace yard was filled with a crowd of nobles and people of all classes, and at their head stood a stately figure that she knew well, with the old velvet gown still flung plaid-wise across the prison dress.

King Siegfried was bidding Schurk deliver up his-ill-gotten power, with the palace and all its treasures, and promising to spare his life if he would do so. But every door and window remained closely barred, and as the king spoke, the tramp tramp of regular soldiers was heard, as regiment after regiment marched up and surrounded them. Then the palace door opened, and out stepped Schurk in the midst of his attendants. " Fire on them, soldiers !" he cried. " Fire on the crowd ! Down with the rebels !"

At this, the crowd began to brandish such weapons as they had among them, and in another moment there would have been a great fight. But King Siegfried lifted his hand and shouted—

"Friends, be patient ! Wait quietly yet a little longer. Soldiers, lower arms ! There shall no blood be shed this day."

The soldiers knew well that commanding voice, and down went the arms that they had pointed.

" Long live King Siegfried !" shouted Edelherz at the top of his voice.

" Long live King Siegfried !" answered the crowd. And all the soldiers joined in the shout, and beaver hats and soldiers' caps went flying into the air together. And the queen was so excited that she shouted too, and Treu jumped about and barked, and so not a voice was silent except those of Schurk and his attendants.

As soon as he could make his voice heard again, the king said, " Soldiers, form square, and cover all entrances to the palace. My friends, I thank you all for the hearty welcome that you have given me. I know that when some of you thought ill of me it was because you were deceived by false reports. Therefore I freely pardon all who have been concerned in the affairs of the last few months, and I do not wish even to know the names of those who took part against me, for we are all friends now."

On hearing this, all the people and soldiers cheered again.

Then Siegfried said : "Schurk, you too shall be pardoned if you will only confess that the papers which you showed were forged."

Schurk looked round, but all retreat was cut off by the soldiers whom he himself had sent for. He advanced towards Siegfried, who came to meet him ; but, instead of the expected confession, Schurk suddenly drew a hidden dagger and plunged it into the king's breast, crying, "Down with the tyrant !"

There was no response to that cry, only a yell of indignation as fifty strong arms were outstretched to seize Schurk, and as many swords drawn.

"Stop, do not kill him—I am not hurt !" cried the king, drawing out and showing the harmless dagger. It seemed wonderful that he should have escaped, but the reason was that in his haste he had not taken off the velvet gown in which he had gone through the streets that night, lest he should be recognized too soon, but had gathered it up and flung it across his shoulder, and its thick folds had prevented the dagger from so much as grazing his skin.

"Schurk," said the king, "you are banished from our kingdom on pain of death if ever you set foot on it again. Go with him, five of my officers, and see him safely out of our dominions."

The crowd made way for the traitor amid hisses and clenchings of the fist. If it had not been for Siegfried's precaution in sending the officers with him, Schurk would hardly have reached the gates of the town alive.

Meanwhile the king had at last time to greet the queen, his wife; and they entered their own palace once more, followed by the blessings and loud hurrahs of the people.

The banquet that the cook had been so busy preparing was held, after all, that day; but it was Siegfried's friends who sat down to it. At the head of the table sat the king himself, with Queen Holda on his right hand and Edelherz the page on his left. Under the table at her feet lay Treu, and his tail went tap, tap, tap against the floor the whole time, until it was a wonder that there was any wag left in it. But it had plenty of practice in wagging from that day forth.

The queen was robed as a queen should be, and crowned and decked with diamonds; but over the back of her state chair there hung the stained and tattered remnants of her blue velvet gown that had done such good service that day.

The feast was drawing to a close when the king turned to his former page and said—

"Edelherz, I have not forgotten that, before these misfortunes came, I had promised to make you my squire. But although it would seem a bad beginning for the re-elected

king to break his word, I have nevertheless changed my mind
as to what I wish to do for you.   Kneel down, therefore, and
take what I now give you instead of squirehood."

Edelherz obeyed, wondering, and the king said, striking
him lightly on the shoulder with his sword—

"Arise, Sir Edelherz, youngest but not least valiant of my
knights, and receive from the queen's hand the first badge of
an order called the 'Order of the Velvet Scarf,' which I hereby
make in honour of this day."

Then the queen stepped forward and threw a blue velvet
scarf over the shoulder of the astonished and delighted young
knight, and fastened it there with a clasp containing her own
and King Siegfried's portraits set in gold.   And all the company applauded, and congratulated the new-made knight,
for the brave and gentle Sir Edelherz was a favourite with
everybody.

But the toast that was received with the greatest applause
that day was one in honour of Queen Holda's beggarly old
blue velvet gown.

PRINCE SILVESTRO'S HOME

VIII.—DIDDLEDY DIDDLEDY DUMPTY.

" Diddledy diddledy Dumpty,
The cat ran up the plum-tree !
Half a crown
To fetch her down,
Diddledy diddledy Dumpty !"

THERE was once a very large and beautiful cat named Purrerita. She was brought up in a king's palace, she curled herself to sleep on the royal throne, and wandered in the palace gardens, and was fed and caressed by royal hands, and had everything that cat could wish. One day the queen said, as puss was purring sleepily on her knee, "Ah, Purrerita ! you are very fond of me as long as I give you all you want ; but if a time should come when you had to serve me instead of I you, I wonder whether you would do it, or whether you would not rather go after the first person who offered you cream to drink."

Purrerita opened her eyes wide, for she felt rather indignant at this speech, but then she thought, "The queen has all she wants, and I have all I want, and it will always be so ; therefore why should I trouble myself to think what I should do if things were changed ?" And she purred herself to sleep again.

But the very next day the change came. A messenger rode pale and breathless into the palace yard, bringing tidings that the king was slain in battle, and that the people, persuaded by the speeches of men who ought to have known better, had declared that they would not have a baby-king, for the king's little son was only four months old, but they must have a man to rule over them. In vain did the king's councillors proclaim that the best and wisest men in the kingdom should be chosen to govern the land until the prince was old enough to do so himself, and called on the people to do nothing in a hurry ; the tumult only grew louder, and before long a second messenger reached the palace gate, bringing word that the people had chosen for king one Dumpty, whom no one had ever heard of before.

He was such a short, fat man, that he had been named Dumpty, because he was nearly as broad as he was tall. But he had a good loud voice, and he had stood up on a barrel and made a speech to the crowd, in which he said that the money and the land ought to belong to the poor people and not to the rich, which is nonsense, for then they would be the rich people, and would have to give back their goods to their former owners, and so on without end. But it was very natural that the poor people should be pleased at the idea of having everything their own way ; and when Dumpty went on to say that if he were king every man should have a house and garden, and fields of his own, and wages should be doubled, and only the masters should pay taxes, and everything should be cheap, the crowd cheered and threw up their hats, and cried, "Dumpty shall be king! Dumpty shall be king!" Immediately he had himself proclaimed as King Dedittodemizo; but nobody in the kingdom could pronounce such a name as that; so before his face they only said Your Majesty, or O King, but behind his back everybody called him Diddledy Dumpty, which was as near as they could get to it, and did just as well.

The queen was like one stunned with the terrible news brought by the two messengers, and before she could recover herself so as to think what to do, came a third rushing with terrified face into the very room where the queen sat, crying, "Fly, madam, fly! Diddledy Dumpty and all his men are marching into the town, and they are coming to take possession of the palace, and to drive out all the servants, and to kill you and the little prince, lest you should dispute the crown with him."

It is not likely that they really meant to kill the queen, but every one in the palace believed it, and there was crying and running about, everybody asking what was to be done, and nobody knowing what to do.

"It's as likely as not they will kill us too," sobbed the housemaid-in-chief. "When once they begin there's no knowing where they will stop."

Then the lamentations rose louder than ever, and one said, "Harness the royal carriages and put the queen and prince into them, and flee." But another said, "No, for they would be known and stopped." And a brave and loyal farmer who was in the town brought his covered van to the door, and offered to carry away the queen in it to his own farm. So they took her up, for she was half swooning, to carry her into it.

"The prince, the prince!" she said; "fetch the prince."

"Yes, yes, they are gone to fetch him," replied her ladies. And then the sound of the drums and trumpets came down the street, and they put her into the van with all speed, and some of her attendants jumped in after her, and the rest ran away, some one way and some another, and the baby was left behind; for the first lady-in-waiting thought that the head nurse would be sure to look after him, so she took up the queen's jewel-case instead, and ran out with it. The head nurse thought that the nursery maid would take him, so she filled her arms with the queen's robes of state, and ran out with them. And the nursery maid was so frightened that she thought of nothing but to run away—away through the fields until the sound of the trumpets and noise of the shouting were left behind in the distance.

There was another inhabitant of the palace who had also been forgotten. Purrerita perceived that there was something unusual going on that morning, so she went up on to the roof, which was a favourite haunt of hers, she had such a good view from it over all the town. Besides, she had always a lingering hope that she might some day catch one of the swallows that flew round her there. From this high post she saw the messengers arriving, and the band of men, with Diddledy Dumpty at their head, approaching in the distance. "The king must be coming home," said Purrerita. "My mistress will be pleased, and then there will be a feast, and I shall get a fine supper of fish." The band of men came nearer and entered the town, and then there was a great running to and fro in the palace, and Purrerita saw the queen carried out, and all the servants scattering hither and thither.

"Dear me! dear me!" she cried, jumping up. "There is something very wrong; it's time I should bestir myself."

And she came scampering down the stairs, looking in at all rooms she passed to see if there was anybody left. And lo! in the nursery lay little Prince Silvestro, asleep in his crib of ivory and gold, with no one to wait upon him. Such a thing had never happened before.

"There must be something very wrong indeed," cried Purrerita, and catching the little prince up by the clothes she ran on with him. There was no time to lose. King Dumpty was coming in by the front entrance, and out dashed Purrerita by the garden door, down the terrace, across the grass-plat, and up with one spring into the fork of a magnificent plum-tree that grew there, in whose thick leafy screen she was soon hidden, baby and all, from any prying eyes. Purrerita knew the tree well, for she had often taken her midday sleep in this green arbour, keeping one eye half open all the time, on the chance of spying some stray robin or chaffinch. She knew of a spot where the branches interlaced so closely that she could lay the baby down without fear, and there she cradled him and watched beside him, until the baby, who had been startled, as well he might be, by such a strange and sudden journey, gave up staring about him, and went off to sleep again, rocked by the swaying of the branches.

"You are a wonderful baby for not crying," thought Purrerita, "and it is well that you are, for if you had cried just now I don't know what would have become of us. Now ·I will steal down and see if I can learn what is become of my mistress."

Very stealthily did she creep across the garden and into the palace. All was confusion there, all the faces strange. In the banqueting hall there was a noisy feast going on, and on the throne at the head of the table there sat a little fat man, who looked all body and no legs.

"Ah, there's a cat!" he screamed, as soon as he saw Purrerita. "Turn her out; I hate cats! Sh-sh-sh, get out with you!" And Purrerita disappeared only just in time to avoid a heavy silver cup that was sent flying after her. She went towards the servants' offices, hoping to find somebody she knew there; but no, all were changed. However, she perceived the dairy door ajar, and carried off a can of fresh milk with her to the plum-tree. She fed the baby with it as soon as he woke, after which he slept quietly until morning. But Purrerita spent a very anxious night. "What will become of us?" she thought. "It's worse, a great deal, than watching at a rat-hole. Suppose the prince should fall down. Suppose he should cry. Suppose I should not be able to find food for him. Really, if the queen does not come home to-morrow, I don't know what I shall do next."

After giving him the remainder of the milk next morning, and watching him until he slept again, Purrerita left the tree in search of food and news. But she found neither, except, indeed, a few bones that served for her own breakfeast; and getting at last terribly uneasy, she ran back to the plum-tree to see whether all was right. She had not observed Diddledy Dumpty sitting in the queen's drawing-room window, but he saw her, and immediately came fussing out into the garden, crying, "There's the cat! there's that cat again! I saw her— she ran up the plum-tree. Go and catch her, somebody. I won't have cats in my garden. Go and catch her, I say."

But the servants who had come running at his call stood and looked at one another, and nobody stirred.

"What! are you afraid?" cried Dumpty—"afraid of a cat? What cowards! Come, half a crown to whoever will fetch her down. Who will win it?"

One of the footmen stepped forward and swung himself cautiously up on the first branch.

"Sssssss!" hissed Purrerita, in a terrible fright, with her tail swelled nearly as big as her body, and she bounced on to another branch so violently that several unripe plums came rattling down, one of them hitting the man on the nose.

"Come back! come back!" cried the others. "She's a witch-cat; she's pelting us with black stones." And they all ran away to a safe distance.

"You great cowards!" said Dumpty. "Fetch me a chair and I will catch her." And he scrambled up on to it and reached up his hand to lay hold of her. But Purrerita, with another great hiss, gave him a mighty scratch, and he came rolling to the ground bellowing.

"Oh, oh, oh! she has wounded me—she will come after me

—help me away ! the wound is poisoned—it's swelling up—
I shall die of it—oh, oh, oh !"

As soon as he got on to his legs, he ran up and down the
terrace, repeating, " Half a crown to fetch her down ! I'll have
her shot—I'll have the tree blown up ! Fetch me a doctor,
somebody ! Half a crown to fetch her down !"

And the boys peeped at him over the garden wall, and
made a song about it that was soon a favourite through all the
town :

> " Diddledy diddledy Dumpty,
> The cat ran up the plum-tree,
> Half a crown
> To fetch her down
> Diddledy diddledy Dumpty !"

" Half a crown to fetch me down !" said Purrerita, smoothing
down her tail to something more like its proper size. " Well,
if you don't get me down, may be it will cost you a whole
crown." And she was so pleased with herself for making this
very clever remark, that it quite restored her to her usual
good temper, and she felt able to look matters in the face
again.

"It won't do to stay here, that's pretty plain," she said.
"But where shall I take him to ? If I had any one to leave
with him while I went to look for a retreat——"

"Leave him with me," said a low humming voice, and looking round, Purrerita saw a bee hovering near her.

"With you ! How could you protect him ?" replied she,
looking with some scorn at a creature so much smaller than
herself.

"I can sting, I can sting," hummed the bee. "I can soothe him to sleep if he frets, I can feed him with bee bread and honey. Only let me fly home to my queen and get her leave to come and watch over him for the rest of the day. Or go yourself and ask our queen if I may be trusted."

"Nay, if you are an obedient subject I can trust you to be an honest friend," said Purrerita. "Go quickly, good bee, for time presses."

The bee darted off, and presently returned, humming joyfully. "Our queen has told off ten to watch and twenty to feed," she hummed. "And she bids me say that since our prince can be served, she will put off our going to wait on him."

"Why, where were you going to?" said Purrerita.

"The king is dead, the queen is fled," returned the bee. "We cannot stay with the new master; he is unpleasant, he is dirty. Therefore we were to swarm to-morrow, to fly to the forest a home to borrow——"

"The forest! that gives me an idea," interrupted Purrerita. "You and your companions keep watch here. I will be back as fast as I can."

The day passed without any one coming near the plum-tree again, for King Dumpty was gone to bed with his scratched hand, and spent his time in bathing it. The bees flew humming round the baby-prince, feeding him with sweet honey and bee bread, and the leaves whispered and rustled as though they knew what an important charge they had confided to their care.

The sun had set before Purrerita came back, but when she crossed the lawn to the plum-tree, it was with her head high and her tail upright and stiff, like a cat that has made up her mind. She found the sentinel bees resting on twigs round the sleeping prince, and waving their wings gently to keep themselves awake.

"Go home to your queen," said Purrerita, "and tell her we go to the forest to-morrow, and that if she will rise betimes and follow, I have found a home both for her and for us."

Very early the next morning, before any one was stirring in palace or town, Purrerita stole slowly and cautiously down the plum-tree, carrying the prince. He was so accustomed to her now that he let her do what she liked with him, and laughed and pulled at her fur with his soft round hands, while Purrerita crept along by the most hidden paths, halting at every sound, and trembling when only a bird stirred in the hedge. With the first ray of sunshine, forth came all the bees from their hive, and with their queen at their head they flew over the palace railings and away until they joined Purrerita at the edge of the forest. Here there was little fear of discovery, for the deer and the squirrels would not tell if they could, and the little company of fugitives continued their journey more boldly down the sunlit glades and through the tangled underwood.

But the prince was heavy, very heavy, Purrerita soon began to think. And then he got tired and cried, and his clothes slipped round so that she could not hold him properly, and then he went to sleep and felt heavier than ever. So it was quite evening before they reached the home that she had chosen. It was a large hollow tree, so large that several people might have sat in the chamber that it formed within its trunk. There were several stories, as it were. Purrerita and the prince took the ground floor; then came the swarm of bees; above them lived a family of squirrels; and two wood-pigeons had built their nest in the branches overhead. The floor in the hollow trunk was dry and soft enough to form a bed for the baby-prince, and all creatures in the forest joined to guard and serve him.

The bees flew humming in and out, laden with sweet food for him; the birds brought offerings of eggs, and the squirrels of nuts; the winds blew softly round the grey old tree, lest they should disturb the child's slumbers; the ivy twined and matted its long streamers across the entrance, to hide and protect the little royal guest; and the sunlight itself glided mellowed through the leafy screen to kiss his brow. It was a strange home, and they were strange nurses for so young a child; but Prince Silvestro grew and prospered under their care. Soon the embroidered robes were all too small for him to wear, and Purrerita was forced to make him a rough garment from the skins of the small animals which she hunted for her own support. By-and-by he began to crawl, and then to walk; and by the time that spring came round he was almost as merry and active, Purrerita thought, as a real kitten could have been.

The boy throve in that free, open-air life, and, as time went on, he grew into a noble-looking little fellow, brown-skinned and straight-limbed, who could run like a cat, climb like a squirrel, and swim like a frog. And Purrerita watched, and was not satisfied. A new thought had occurred to her, and made her anxious. Suppose the queen were to come home at last, and when she brought her boy to her, she were to take him on her knee and speak to him, as she surely would, what would he answer her? He could talk with birds and bees, and all the wild creatures in the forest, but of human speech he knew not a word: how should he? Then the queen would lay the fault to her, Purrerita thought, and would say that she had ill fulfilled her charge; and what was to be done? She knew no human being with whom she dared to share her secret and her forest home; or if she had, who would come so far for the coaxing of a cat?

"I will go once more to the palace, and see whether there is any news of the queen," said Purrerita. "It is more than a month since I was there. And I can at least take counsel with old Bigotado, the stable cat; he used to be reckoned a wise old fellow."

Before daybreak she was up and on her way. From her favourite perch in the plum-tree she saw Diddledy Dumpty sitting at breakfast with his lords. The windows were open on account of the heat, and she could hear how they were laughing and amusing themselves with a grey parrot that had lately been sent to Dumpty. As she listened to the parrot's ready speech and witty answers, a thought came into Purrerita's head which set her off purring louder than she had done for a long while. The parrot was the very helper that she wanted ! What if she could persuade him to come and teach Prince Silvestro to talk ? Down jumped Purrerita from the plum-tree, and gliding unnoticed into the room, she hid herself in the boughs of a myrtle that stood in its pot close to the gilded pole to which the parrot was chained.

She waited until Dumpty and his companions were talking loudly among themselves, and then called softly, "Sir Bavardin! Sir Bavardin!" for she had observed that this was the name by which he was addressed.

"Who calls me ?" said the parrot, putting his head on one side, and glancing about him.

"A friend," replied Purrerita, who asks you whether you would not like to be free to fly as you may please, and yet have a home to shelter you from all weather ?"

"To be sure I should!" said Bavardin. "This must be some lady of my tribe," he added, to himself, "who has seen me by chance, and who evidently finds something in me to admire." And he seated himself very upright on his pole.

"I can offer you such a home," continued Purrerita, "on condition that you will become professor of language to a noble pupil."

"Ah! she has a son," said the parrot to himself, "whom she wishes to make as clever and accomplished as I am. Dear lady," he added, aloud, "I accept the condition."

"You promise to come, then ?" said Purrerita.

"If I can but get free from this chain," answered Bavardin. "I give you my word, as I am a parrot of honour. Witness my claw!" For you must know that he had lived with a

I

lawyer for three years, and so was very learned in all business matters.

"Then," said Purrerita, "meet me in the plum-tree yonder as soon as possible. If you can but get there I will manage the rest." And she stole away again to the tree.

"Amiable stranger, my life is at your disposal!" said Bavardin, who did not perceive that she was already gone. Then, drooping his wings and ruffling his plumes, he put on the most dejected air imaginable; and when the company turned to talk to him again, he would not answer a word.

"What is the matter with Bavardin?" said Dumpty. "He is turned sulky."

"Oh no, master," said Bavardin. "I am dying for want of a little fresh air."

"Stuff and nonsense," said Dumpty. "Fresh air never did any one good yet. However, my lord high sheriff, you may as well undo his chain, and carry him out for a turn; but hold him fast, mind."

My lord high sheriff looked as if he did not much fancy the job, and he held the parrot so daintily, that a single sharp peck from his hooked beak was enough, and Bavardin was free. Away he flew to the plum-tree, where Purrerita met him with open arms. But when he saw what she was, Bavardin fell back with a screech.

"Treachery!" he cried. "Fair one who promised to meet me, where are you?"

"Here, to be sure," said Purrerita, clapping her paw on him, for he looked very much as if he were going to fly away again. "Why, what's the matter now? Don't you want to come?"

"Ye—ye—yes," stammered the parrot.

"Then what are you shaking like that for? If you repent of your promise, say so."

"Oh no, I will come with the gr—greatest pleasure," replied Bavardin; which was not true, only he thought if he seemed unwilling to come she would most likely bite his head off.

"Come on, then," said Purrerita. "Don't you hear what a fuss they are making under the tree already?"

But Bavardin seemed too frightened to stir, whereupon Purrerita caught him up in her mouth, and making a dash for it, she scampered past king and courtiers, and all, and over the wall and away, before Dumpty had time to do more than cry, "Oh, the cat! the cat was up the plum-tree again! She's stolen my parrot! Oh, do kill her, somebody!"

And the courtiers looked fierce, and rushed about, but they had no mind to come near her for fear of getting scratched; and Dumpty himself was too fat to run, so that Purrerita might have taken it easily enough if she had known.

When she reached the skirts of the forest, she set Bavardin down, and he shook his ruffled plumage and said—

"You hurt me."

"It was your own fault," said Purrerita. "What did you struggle so for? Remember another time that you may screech as much as you please, only do not flap your wings about."

"Catch me in your mouth again, and I promise you I will stir neither wing nor claw," returned the parrot, gaily, for he was a good-tempered fellow, and had a very good habit of making the best of things. So they travelled the rest of their journey side by side, like good friends.

Bavardin did not repent his coming, although he had been taken aback a little at the first. He found Prince Silvestro so apt a pupil, that it was quite a pleasure to teach him ; for the young prince, when he heard that this was the language of human beings like himself, never rested content until he had learnt all that Bavardin could teach him. Then he began questioning him. What were people like ? How did they live ? What did they do ? and Bavardin, who enjoyed nothing so well as a good gossip, would tell him long stories, for hours together, of all that he had seen and heard.

Purrerita, as she lay watching the two, would rejoice over her clever plan, and purred softly to herself, spreading her claws out and drawing them in again, while she thought, "Now my prince is perfect. Now he is fit to mix with other people, to govern his kingdom. If only the queen would come for him !"

If she had known all that was going on in the prince's mind, perhaps Purrerita would not have rejoiced so greatly in Bavardin's coming. For Prince Silvestro was as one awaked from sleep by Bavardin's stories of men. Up to this time the companionship of birds and bees and the wild creatures of the forest had been enough for him ; he had spent his time, like them, in climbing and playing, and getting food, and had been content. But now he longed for something more, something different, he hardly knew what. People were evidently something better and higher than the creatures he knew; they understood the reason of things, and that was just what he was longing to know. For Bavardin, though he could tell stories without end, could explain nothing. Purrerita was better than he, yet she had nothing to answer when he asked such questions as, What were all things made for? Who made them? How did all creatures know how to build their nests and get their food, when nobody taught them? How was it that he himself knew nothing of the sort? And why were men so much wiser than other animals? But when he asked this last question, Bavardin exclaimed, "Oh, I know! It is because of certain little square cases that they have, like boxes, only they are not boxes, for though they have a top and a bottom, they have no sides except at one end. And they are full of layers of white stuff like broad strips of birch-bark, scrawled all over with black marks, just like the eggs of a yellow-hammer. Some men will sit and look at these black scrawls for hours, and the wiser they are the fonder they are of looking at them, for I have heard them say themselves that it is this which makes them wise."

"But how? how can it?" Bavardin could tell no more.

At this time Purrerita told Prince Silvestro who he was, and all that she knew of his mother and of what had happened in the palace. Here was matter for more thought; and the prince, forgetting his climbing and his games, would wander away alone to dream undisturbed, for he tried to satisfy himself by endless day-dreams, in which his mother figured as a being something between Purrerita and the queen-bee, and the rest of his people were to match. For Prince Silvestro had only once seen two men, and that was a long way off, for Purrerita had taught him to flee from man as from creatures more to be feared than wolves ; and though he had begun to think that she must be mistaken, men came so seldom into that part of the forest, that the days and weeks went by and he had no opportunity of learning whether his idea or Purrerita's was most right.

But what had become of the queen all this long time? When she fled that day from the palace, the farmer who had offered to hide the queen took her to his own farm. It was not until they reached it that the terrible discovery was made that the prince had been left behind. Then there was weeping and lamenting, and those of the queen's servants who still clung to her went from house to house through all the town, looking for him. They examined every baby, they even made their way into the palace to search for him. But nobody thought of looking up the plum-tree, so the little prince was not found, and one after another they came back sadly to the farm.

Then the queen said that it was all her own fault, for that she ought to have looked after him and not trusted to others. And she took it so to heart that for some time they feared she would have died of grief.

Now the farmer had a little baby girl, of nearly the same age as the lost prince. They tried to keep her out of the way, thinking that the sight of her would distress the queen by reminding her of her own baby; but one day the queen heard her crying, and went to her, and it seemed as if the care and attention that were needed in tending the child did her good instead of harm. From that day forth she always took charge of the child while her own mother was busy with the house-work, and the little thing, as soon as she could speak, always called the queen her lady-mother. Little Alegria was the brightest, merriest little maid that ever gladdened a household. Her sweet temper made her a favourite with everybody, and her delight was to help and cheer all around her. But she could not cheer the queen, for the thought of her little lost son was always before her.

One day, as Alegria stood by the farmer's chair as he finished his breakfast, she said, "Father, why is my lady-mother always so sad?"

"Because she once had a little son, who was born about the same time that you were, and she has lost him," said the farmer.

"But when people die," returned Alegria, "do they not go to a beautiful place where they are always happy? Then why should that make her sad?"

"Ah! but she does not know whether he is alive or dead, or what has become of him," said the farmer. "She lost him, as I say; she was ill, and left him for somebody else to take who did not take him, and so she feels as if · it were in a manner her own fault."

Alegria stood silent for a few minutes; then she said, "Father, I will go and find her son."

"Ay, child, if you could do that," returned the farmer, stroking her hair, "it were a glad day for us all." Then he went to see that all his out-houses and stables were put into good repair before winter came on, little thinking what effect his last words had had.

For little Alegria looked upon them as a permission to her to go and seek for this lost son and bring him home ; and full of eager hope, she wrapped her little blue mantle about her, and set forth at once. Who could tell ? the little boy might be coming along the lane at that moment, crying for want of his mother. Or he might be kept a prisoner in some wicked man's house, and be dying because no one came to set him free. Full of these thoughts, she passed through the fields and down the road, looking right and left as she went, and inquiring at every house that she passed.

She was not missed at home till the evening, for her father and mother thought she was with the queen, and the queen thought she was with them, so that she had a good start before the search for her began.

Her bright face and winning ways gained her a night's lodging at a distant farm, and the next morning she was early on her way again. She turned out of the road to call at the house of a woodman, and then took a way that led through some trees. But the trees grew thicker round her, and no cottage or sign of man was to be seen ; and by-and-by, when she came to the end of a glade, her path, or what she had taken for a path, ceased altogether. She tried to find its continuation in several directions, and then thought she would go back by the way she came ; but by this time she was so bewildered that even that was impossible, and Alegria had to make her way on through the thicket, frightened sometimes by the wild cries of the birds or the whirr of a startled pheasant, but still keeping up a good heart and pushing forward.

Meantime the sky grew dark overhead ; there was a storm coming, and every leaf and twig was still, as if watching breathless for what would happen. The first big drops were pattering down, when Alegria heard a rushing as of water, and turned towards it. Perhaps there would be a path beside it, or at least an opening in the high tangle that did not let her see more than a few feet before her. A violent gust of wind came down, and the branches creaked and swayed ; then came another, and a clap of thunder with it, and at the same time Alegria felt the matted bushes under her feet give way,—she was slipping, falling into the torrent that foamed beneath. Clinging fast to the bushes, she screamed aloud for help, with little hope indeed of being heard, when a voice answered her, a strong arm grasped her, and she found herself standing on firm land again, with a bright-eyed boy beside her, clad in rabbit-skins, who pushed aside the brambles and led her forward, smiling and promising her shelter from the storm.

That was a winter that was remembered in that country for many years ; for after the thunderstorm came a change of weather. The snow fell thick and fast, a bitter frost set in, and weeks and months went by, and the snow remained unmelted. Never had such a winter been known. The roads were impassable ; people dug a way through the deep snow to their cowhouses and barns, and in the towns men had to work with spade and shovel almost daily to keep the thoroughfares open.

In the forest, indeed, the squirrels slept soundly, curled up in their cosy nests ; the birds crept into holes and sheltered nooks ; everything seemed to slumber. But in the old hollow tree all was lively and wakeful enough. The very thickness of the snow made it warm and snug within, and Prince Silvestro hollowed it out and heaped it up into another chamber at the entrance, lined with branches of pine and fir. The floor was spread with a carpet of dried bracken, and a column of blue wood-smoke rose night and day from a fireplace of loose stones, before which Purrerita lay and licked herself lazily, purring for pleasure. On a perch close beside her sat Bavardin ; he was the only inhabitant of the hollow tree who was not quite contented, for he thought that since Alegria had come, Prince Silvestro had rather neglected his conversation for hers. Besides, he had for some time been wishing for a wider sphere in which to exercise his talents, as he put it, meaning thereby more people to talk to. Prince Silvestro and Alegria had not been long together before she discovered that she had found her lady-mother's son, and he, that he had as good as found the mother who had for so long been the subject of his dreams. And his face lost its wistful, perplexed look, and the expression of his eyes grew deeper, for now he knew the meaning of all that had puzzled him so before ; why he was in the world, and what his work was, and who it was that ruled everything so wonderfully, and taught those creatures by instinct that had not sense enough to learn in any other way. Alegria, who had been taught by the queen herself, was a wise little maiden, and enjoyed teaching the young prince all that she knew. So the time did not seem long to any of them while they waited until the roads should be passable again.

At last the south wind blew, the rain fell, and the snow melted, leaving behind it a sea of mud and mire, until the sun, shining at last from a cloudless sky, had power to dry it up.

With the first warm spring days a strange procession was seen wending its way from the depths of the forest towards the town in which the royal palace stood. In the middle walked a princely boy, clad from head to foot in skins. On one side of him came a smiling little maiden in a blue mantle, and on the other a cat trotted soberly along, as befitted her age and dignity, but with her head and tail erect and her whiskers well forward. Perched on the boy's shoulder, or fluttering above his head, there was a grey parrot, who seemed almost beside himself with joy, for he chattered and screamed, and whistled and chattered again, without once stopping to draw breath. Above him again came a whole colony of bees flying like a cloud, each swarm headed by its separate queen. Along the hedgerows on either side of the road leaped and scampered little brown squirrels, that kept pace with the party in the middle, as did a company of little birds of all kinds that flew with much twittering from tree to tree.

And as they passed, the people all came out of their houses

and followed in the rear. But one, who recognized little Alegria, mounted his horse and rode to her home to carry the news with such speed, that by the time they reached the entrance of the town, the farmer and his wife and the queen came out to meet them.

Then there was such a meeting as it would be hard to describe. The people round them shouted, "Long live the Queen! Long live the Prince, our little king!" And all the country rose up as one man and brought them to the palace. For they had long ago found out that Diddledy Dumpty's promises were worth nothing, and worse than nothing ; for his government had so upset the country, that trade had sunk and prices had risen, and many men were ruined, and they were longing for an opportunity to go back to the old state of things.

It was Diddledy Dumpty's turn to run away now ; and in spite of his short legs and his fat body he did run away so fast and far that nobody in the country heard of him again during all the long and prosperous reign of King Silvestro.

When the royal party entered the palace, Purrerita, forgetting altogether her age and dignity, dashed like a mad thing out of the window, down the terrace, across the grass-plot, and up the plum-tree. There she sat purring, full of contentment, while all the young leaves round her whispered and rustled for joy.

THE MONEY-WOMAN.

Page 125.

IX.—SEE-SAW, MARGERY DAW.

MARGERY DAW, Johnny's mother, lived in as poor a cottage as it is possible for any one to live in. There were holes in the moss-grown thatch, and holes in the damp clay floor, holes in the mud-built walls, and as to the windows, they were hardly anything else but holes. She would not have stayed there if she could have helped it; for of course it was terribly cold and draughty; but although she took in washing from the neighbouring town, and worked hard all the week, it was as much as she could do to pay the rent even of that miserable little cottage. But her little boy Johnny was a merry little fellow, although he ran about barefooted and bareheaded, and as for playthings, he never had had so much as a ball or a marble in his life. But he had what was much better—a playfellow. His little cousin Margery Daw— she was not a very near relation, although she had the same name, being fifth cousin three times removed—she was his constant playfellow.

Little Margery had been left quite alone in the world, so Johnny's mother, poor as she was, took Margery home to her cottage and brought her up, together with Johnny. There was no end to the games that they played together. They drove coaches, or they were runaway horses, or they carried thistles and ragwort-heads to market, and sold them to one another for turnips and cauliflowers. But their favourite playground was a piece of land close by belonging to Farmer Shepperley, where he had left a number of stems of trees to season. They were flung about anyhow, one across the other, and Johnny and Margery clambered about among them, and sat underneath them, and walked along them. And it is no such easy thing, mind you, to walk along a slippery tree-stem that is raised partly off the ground. It is all very well as long as you are on the thick part, but when you come to the small end that noddles about and sways up and down under your feet, first you begin to run, and then you feel that you *must* jump off to save yourself from falling, so it is not often that you get to the tip. There was one tree in particular, that was so nicely balanced across a fat trunk that the weight of Johnny or Margery was enough to swing it up and down. Such games of see-saw they had on it! Johnny gave Margery the broad end because she was a girl, and he himself mounted on the narrow one, and they flew up and down, and tumbled off, and laughed and shouted and tumbled off again, until every one that passed by must have longed to come and play at see-saw with them.

Little Margery was richer than Johnny, for she had something of her own. It was a bed, a nice spring mattress, with a little iron bedstead painted green, and with brass knobs at the four corners, and a baby's face in bright brass in the middle of the foot-piece, and another in the middle of the head. It had been left to her by her grandmother; and of course when Margery came to live with Johnny's mother she brought her bed with her. There is a nursery rhyme about Margery and her bed, but it is not at all a pretty one. It says—

> " See-saw, Margery Daw
> Sold her bed, and lay upon straw.
> Was not she a dirty slut
> To sell her bed and lie upon dirt ?"

But it is not fair to call Margery such ugly names, for this is why she sold her bed. Towards the end of the spring Johnny's mother fell ill. The days went on and she did not get any better, and one morning Johnny said to her : " Mother, when people are ill they have a doctor. Why should you not have one ?"

" My dear, I should be very glad to have a doctor," she answered, "but a doctor must be paid, and I have got no money to pay him."

Now little Margery was busy sweeping just outside the door, and heard what they said. And she thought to herself, " How I should like to get enough money to pay for a doctor !" And then a thought struck her, and she went softly in, and washed her hands and smoothed her hair and put on her shoes, for she did not wear them about the house for fear of wearing them out. Then she took her little green bedstead, and pulled it out at the door, and away in the direction of the town.   It had very good castors, so when once she had got it over the rough bit of lane it went well enough along the path, she pushing at it behind like a perambulator.   And when she reached the town, what a rattling and clattering it did make over the pavement, to be sure!   Everybody turned round to see what was going on, but Margery took no notice of them, and went straight to the door of a shop where she had seen bedsteads for sale.

"Please, sir, will you buy my bedstead?" she said to the shopkeeper, who came out to see what was happening.

"Bless me, no, child!" said the shopman.   "What do you expect to get for it?"

"I don't know," said Margery.   "I want enough to pay the doctor."

"Well, I'll give you ten shillings," said the man.

"That won't do," said Margery, shaking her head.   "I want more than ten shillings."

"More than ten shillings for an old second-hand bed, with half the paint knocked off!" cried the man.   But this was not true, for there was not a bit of paint knocked off.

"Come, come," said a man inside the shop, "give the child a fair price for it."

"Well, Mr. Shepperley, to please you," said the shopkeeper, "I'll give a pound for it, and that's a great deal more than it's worth."

"Oh, thank you!" said Margery, holding out her hand for it.   "And as that is more than it's worth, if some day I bring you back the pound you will give me my bed again, won't you ?"

" Ah, that's fair enough," said Mr. Shepperley again, as the shopkeeper hesitated.

" Well," he said at last, " you might have it if I've not sold it in the meantime."

" Thank you, sir," said Margery. "But I don't suppose I shall ever get it back," she thought, as she walked away ; "for I don't think I am likely ever to get a pound again, unless perhaps when I grow up to be a woman However, I'm glad I did it ; and here is the doctor's door."

Margery left a message asking him to call, and then ran to the grocer's shop, where she bought a quarter of a pound of tea, half a pound of sugar, and one candle. Then to the draper's, where she bought a blanket. All these things together cost seven shillings and threepence farthing, so she had a good handful of shillings left as she trudged home.

The doctor soon came, and said he would send a bottle of medicine. And he told Margery to go to the butcher and buy a scrag end of mutton to make broth for the sick woman. So ninepence more of Margery's pound went for that ; and then she came home and put it on in the saucepan, and wrapped Mother Margery, as she called her, in the warm new blanket, and told her all that she had done. And Johnny's mother kissed her, and said that she was a dear good little girl.

When Johnny came home and heard about it, he hardly knew whether to be most glad that his mother had had the

K

doctor, or most sorry that Margery had sold her precious bed.

"It ought to be I who should be getting the money and paying for things," he said to himself; "but I am so little, nobody will believe how hard I can work, and I don't suppose I shall get another threepence all the summer. Oh dear! what shall I do?"

Johnny was not quite without something to do, for an old weaver who lived near had shown him a box, and told him that when he could fill that box with tufts of sheep's wool, picked off the hedges and brambles, he would give him three-pence. Twice during the winter Johnny had filled that box, but now warm weather was come, and the sheep had all been shorn, and not a tuft of wool was to be found, though he wandered all the next day through the fields and up and down the hedges. The next morning he went out again in another direction; still no wool. Poor Johnny sat down under the hedge and was just going to cry, when he heard the pleasant sound of the whetting of scythes.

"Haymaking is going to begin!" thought he, and scrambling up the bank he saw a row of mowers bending to their work, and their scythes passing with a smooth swish through the soft thick grass. Then he saw a group of women in hats, or with their bonnets cocked very much over their noses, and rakes in their hands, going into the adjoining field to turn over the grass that had already been cut. Lastly he saw Farmer Shepperley himself coming up to the gate to see how his men got on. And when Johnny saw him, he suddenly slipped down off the bank and set off running to meet him as fast as his legs would carry him. He caught him before he got to the mowers.

"Oh, sir," cried Johnny, nearly breathless, "mother's sick and I'm sure I could help to make hay."

"Eh, what!" said the farmer. "A little whippersnapper like you? Why, they would rake you up in a truss of hay, and never know you were there."

"No, but they shouldn't," said Johnny, "because I would kick and call out. Please let me try, sir. You don't know how strong I am. I can lift the big kettle."

"Well, you seem to be a sharp little chap," said the farmer, "and I don't mind trying you if you will work hard. But mind, I shall give you only a penny a day, because you can work no faster. Go and see what you can do behind the women there."

Away ran Johnny, well pleased, and very hard did he work all day. He did not go home to dinner, for he had taken a bit of bread in his pocket, and the head mower gave him a piece of his slice of cheese for finding his hone for him that he had lost. One of the women too gave him an old hat of her little boy's, because she said he would get a sun-stroke, working bare-headed. When evening came Johnny's legs and arms were aching and one of his hands was blistered, but he never thought about that when the farmer gave him his penny and told him he might come again to-morrow.

The grass would have had to be uncommonly quick to have grown under Johnny's feet as he went home that night. He burst into the cottage, holding up his penny and crying, "Look, mother! Margery, look! Mother, I've got a new master and

I'm to have only a penny a day, because I can work no faster."

He put the penny into his mother's hand as he spoke. The two Margerys were so pleased they hardly knew what to say, and Johnny felt as if he had quite grown into a man.

The next day he worked again in the hayfield, and the next, and the next. His mother grew better, and was able to get up and stir about in the house again. But by this time all the money that Margery had got for her bed was spent, and Johnny soon found that a penny a day would not keep him and Margery and his mother too.

"I wish I had as much money as I want," he said to himself, as he sat alone on a mossy bank in the hayfield, while the rest of the haymakers were gone home to dinner. "I wish I could buy mother the meat and good food that she ought to have, and the gown that she needs so greatly. I wish I could get back Margery's bed before the shopkeeper sells it. I wish I had a money-woman to give me money whenever I want it. I wish—Holloa! Stop me! Oh!"

He was slipping down through the bank. First his knees disappeared, then his waist, then his shoulders. Down, down, and he could no more stop himself from sinking than if the earth had been made of boiled batter pudding. He felt the ground close over his head, and still down, down in the darkness. Then a light below, his feet struck upon solid ground and he found himself standing in a large high cavern, lighted by a ring all round it of little fires, and upon each fire a pipkin full of something red-hot. The walls of the cavern were scooped out into shelves, which were full of piles of shining money. And in the middle of the ring of fires stood a little old woman, so wonderfully dressed that Johnny took notice of it, scared as he was. She wore a cap of spun silver, with bows and ribbons of gold, a bodice of zinc, a petticoat of bronze, and a good wide apron of tin.

You would suppose that such a dress would make her rather stiff in her movements, but not a bit of it ; she moved about as briskly as if she had been clothed in cotton or brown holland.

"Well," she said, nodding and smiling to Johnny, "here I am, you see."

"Oh," replied Johnny, not quite knowing what to say.

"And you cannot say I've been long in answering your wish."

"But I didn't wish !" cried Johnny, who was not at all pleased to find himself in such a queer place.

"You did, though, just this minute," said the old lady.

"Dear me !" exclaimed Johnny, "are you a money-woman, ma'am ?"

"I am The Money-woman," said the little old lady, drawing herself up ; "there is no other in the world. All the money that you see on those shelves I made over my fires."

"Dear me !" said Johnny, venturing a step forward to look at it. "Do you make all the money in the world ?"

"Bless me, no !" said the Money-woman ; "I only make it for particular purposes. Whenever I see any deserving persons in want of mcney, I supply them with some. But my special delight is, whenever I know of any one who is giving away his money for good and wise and kind purposes, to fill up his purse again all unknown to him. They often wonder, those people, how it is that their money holds out so wonderfully; but I could tell them, if I chose. There's a blessing on it, you see;" and the old lady nodded till her gold cap-ribbons glittered again.

"I wonder whether she will give me some money," said Johnny to himself; but the Money-woman must have heard him, for she said—

"Yes, certainly I will; but do you suppose you have never had anything from me yet? Where do you think the pennies came from that Farmer Shepperley gave you? They were every one of them coined in my mint; he will be none the poorer for their loss!" and the old woman nodded again until her gold cap-ribbons flashed in the firelight. "Now come and see how I coin," she said. "Do you see these passages leading out of my cavern into the heart of the earth? That is Gold Street, this Silver Street, that Copper Street, and so on. Now I take a lump of silver from Silver Street, and put it into this pipkin. Blow the fire a bit—here are the bellows. That's right; now it is melted. Here is my die, with five little round sockets, you see, the size of shillings. First, I must wax it, to prevent the hot silver from sticking. Now I pour it bubbling in, clap on the cover, and put it up the ventilator to cool. In a few minutes they will come out shillings, and you shall have them."

"That's very nice," said Johnny. "Do the mints coin their money in this way?"

"Dear me, no!" said the Money-woman; "theirs is a much clumsier way. They don't half know how to use the precious metals. Why, did you ever see a tin apron before?"

"I don't think I ever did," said Johnny. "Mother wears cotton ones."

"Poor dabby rags!" said the Money-woman. "Ah! I see you're looking at the names above my shelves. See, here is my English money; here is the Australian; there is French; that is German, and so on. Now, how much am I to give you?"

Johnny opened his eyes wide at this question. "Oh, a good lot!" he said.

"How much at a time?"

"Five pounds!" said Johnny, boldly.

"You shall have it if you wish," said the Money-woman; "but I advise you to take only a little, and come again for more. If you have a quantity, people will wonder where you got it from, and you may get into trouble; for of course you will never mention that you have seen me."

"But I want to buy so many things," said Johnny. "I want a dress for mother, and——"

"Well, please yourself," said the Money-woman; "but my advice to you is, take little and often. When you want to come to me, you have only to sit down on the ground, take a buttercup between your finger and thumb, as you did just now on the bank——"

"Did I?" said Johnny. "Dear me, yes! here it is in my hand still."

"You must hold the buttercup as I have told you," continued the Money-woman, "and say, 'I wish I was with my Money-woman;' that's all."

"That won't be very hard to remember," said Johnny.

"And now," added the Money-woman, "you must go, for the dinner hour is over, and the haymakers will be calling for you. What will you take? the five pounds? Be careful then, that's all, and good morning to you.—Off!"

As she said off, Johnny felt his hair lifted as if by a draught of air from beneath, and up he went, straight for the roof of the vault, and in a moment found himself standing in the corner of the hayfield where he had left his rake. His first act was to put his hand into his pocket. There were the five pounds, sure enough. "It's uncommonly jolly!" said he, and ran to rake after the hay-cart.

They worked late that day, for it was the last day of carrying hay, and they stayed to clear it all off. But as soon as work was done, instead of going home, Johnny ran straight to the town. First to the shop where Margery had sold her bed. There it was, safe and sound; and Johnny paid the pound and walked off with it down the street in triumph. Then to the draper's, to buy his mother a gown. Then to the butcher for a leg of mutton. Then to the shoemaker for a pair of shoes for Margery. Then to the grocer's, where he bought tea, sugar, pepper, a box of matches, a pound of candles that did not want snuffing, and a bar of soap. Then off he trotted homewards, driving the bedstead in front of him.

Greatly were the two Margerys amazed to see Johnny

arrive in such style, with the green bedstead and all the things upon it. "But where did you get the money, Johnny? But who gave you the money, Johnny?"

And Johnny nodded knowingly, but answered not a word. "Next time I see the Money-woman I'll ask her to let me tell mother, though," he thought; "it does not seem right to have secrets from her."

"Mother," said Johnny, the next morning, "I can have a go at setting the garden to rights to-day, for the hay is all carried and stacked. But Farmer Shepperley told me that I might come to-morrow if I like, and help weed his potatoes." So Johnny went to work at the garden, and after a bit Margery came out to help him. As for old Margery, she had the leg of mutton to cook. When the evening came, Johnny said, "I say, Margery, let us go and have a game at the see-saw. We've not been near it, I don't know when." Margery was ready enough to go, and a jolly game they had. When they came running home at last, hot and merry, Johnny's mother said, "A neighbour who passed just now told me that your old master, the weaver, is very weak and poorly. Don't you think that a slice off our leg of mutton would be the very thing for him?"

"First-rate," said Johnny, "and I'll take it to-night, for fear I should have no time to-morrow. Only let us have supper first, that you may go to bed without waiting, in case I should be late." And this accordingly was done.

The next day Johnny was tugging away at a big thistle in Farmer Shepperley's potato-field, when he felt a hand on his shoulder, and looking up, saw himself in the grasp of a policeman. Poor Johnny cried out and asked what they wanted with him, for he had done nothing.

"Haven't you though!" said the policeman. "We shall soon see about that. You keep quiet and come along with me, you young rascal!"

So poor Johnny was led through the town and put into prison. There he learned that he was accused of murdering Farmer Shepperley. For the farmer had disappeared, and nobody knew where he was gone. But after a great hunt they had found a pocket-handkerchief of his on a wild boggy bit of land, through which went the road to the hills. And people began to talk of robbery and murder, and of Johnny's sudden and unexplained riches. Then somebody remembered having seen him out late the night before, running by with something hidden under his jacket, which indeed was the basin in which he had carried the slice of mutton to the old weaver.

They had him up before the judge, and the butcher, and the grocer, and the young man at the draper's shop, all came and said how he had been spending money in this and in that, and had been running about the town like a mad fellow with a green iron bedstead and a leg of mutton on the top of it. In that country there was no lawyer appointed to advise the prisoner, as there is with us, so poor Johnny did not know what to answer, except that indeed, indeed, he had not done it.

"Where did you get all that money, then?" said the judge.

"A lady gave it to me."

"What lady?"

"She told me not to tell—I must not tell," said Johnny. "But she did give it to me."

Then the judge shook his head, and said that was a likely story. And the end of it was that Johnny was pronounced guilty and condemned to be hanged.

No Money-woman came forward, as Johnny hoped she might, to explain where he got the money. He thought once of telling the judge about her, for surely he thought she would not mind his doing so to save his life. But when he came to consider it, would they believe his story of the cavern, and the heaps of money, and the old lady in a zinc bodice and bronze petticoat? They would only laugh at it; so there was no help for him.

The day before he was to be hanged, Margery came to see him. She had gone to the judge himself, and begged and begged until he gave her leave. "Dearest Johnny," she said, "is there anything that I can do for you?"

"Yes!" cried Johnny, in a loud voice, for a thought suddenly came to him. "Run to the nearest field and fetch me a buttercup. Run, Margery, for if you succeed it may save my life." Margery was gone without another word, and Johnny sat down to wait for her.

She seemed to have been gone a long time. Perhaps they would not let her in again, and he should never get the buttercup after all. Johnny's eyes filled with tears as he pictured all this to himself; but before they could fall he heard the bolt of his prison-door drawn back, and Margery appeared in the doorway with the jailor behind her.

"I must not come in," she said, "but here are your butter-cups. Good-bye, dear, dear Johnny!" and she was gone.

The moment that the bolt had grated into its place again, Johnny seized his buttercups, sat down on the floor, and said, "I wish I was with my Money-woman!"

Before he could draw breath the prison was left behind, and Johnny stood safe in the firelit cavern. Why, where was his Money-woman? She was not in the middle of her fires, but as he looked round she came hurrying up a passage, dressed in an aluminium bonnet, a brass shawl with a fringe of steel filings, and a big copper umbrella in her hand. Johnny darted up to her, and taking hold of a corner of her brass shawl, told her all his story.

"Dear, dear, dear, dear!" said the Money-woman, when he had finished. "It doesn't answer, you see; it doesn't answer. And here was I, who ought to have been looking after you, called away to Australia on urgent business. It is a long way there and back, because I cannot take the short cut straight through the middle of the earth, on account of the centre of gravity, you know. And there are so many hidden volcanoes about just now that I was obliged to take my umbrella for fear of a shower of ashes. Well, well, well! and what shall we do now? for you can't go back; no, you can't go back. I'll tell you what!" she exclaimed. "Suppose you stay here and help me. I have more to do than I can rightly get through, and they won't come here to look for you."

Johnny thought he should like this very much; but how about mother?

The Money-woman had a plan for her too. "Of course you will go and see her this evening," she said, "and you shall take her some money, and tell her to go and hire a certain cottage that I know of in a lonely glen; it is ever so much better than her present one. And you and I will go and tidy it up and make it comfortable for her, and she and Margery shall go and live there, and you can be with them as much as you please. There, never mind about thanks, but blow that fire for me (bless me, how soon they get low!) while I go and see whether the coast is clear for you to visit your mother."

The two Margerys, sitting sad and lonely in their tumble-down cottage, never saw the Money-woman as she peeped at them, still in her aluminium bonnet, through a hole in the wall. But they saw quick enough when Johnny came tumbling in, laughing, crying, hugging, and telling them some wonderful rigmarole about a new cottage and an old lady in a tin apron, all in one breath. He went back again, however, to spend the night with the Money-woman, for fear of getting taken to prison a second time.

The fuss that there was in that prison the next morning is not to be told. They hunted, they shouted, they ran about, they poked under the straw that had been given him for his bed, but no Johnny. The crowd were assembled, everything was ready, but no Johnny. Then there was a great kick-up. The jailor turned off the turnkeys, and the judge turned off the jailor, and the mob broke the judge's windows, and when the uproar was at the highest, who should they see coming as cool as could be down the street, at the tail of a flock of sheep, but Farmer Shepperley himself. There was a great shout, and everybody rushed to ask him what it all meant; and so, as might have been expected, instead of getting an answer, they only succeeded in knocking him down. So then they picked him up and took him to the judge, and begged him to question him.

Been? Farmer Shepperley had only been to a farm far away over the moors, to buy a flock of sheep.

"But why did you tell nobody where you were going?" asked the judge.

"Of course I was not going to let all the other farmers know. Why they'd have been coming up wanting to buy them too, and the price would have been doubled. So I just slipped away unbeknownst. And as for my pocket-handkerchief, the wind blew it away out of my hand, and it was so dark, and the ground so boggy, that I could not get it back."

Then they told him about Johnny, and how they had suspected the boy of murdering him; and Farmer Shepperley was very sorry he had been put in prison, and very glad he had got out again, and would they please to let him go and look after his sheep, or they would be wandering all over the country. And so, as there was nothing more to get from him, they let him go.

When the Money-woman, who had her own ways of learning all that was going on, told Johnny how Farmer Shepperley had come back safe and sound, he was very glad to hear it, but said that he would rather stay with his Money-woman than go back to work on the top of the earth again, even if they did not want to hang him any longer. The Money-woman replied that in that case she must set to work and make him a suit of clothes, which she did that very evening, and the next morning Johnny was strutting proudly about in a zinc jacket and waistcoat with brass buttons, a pair of bronze trousers, and a little tin apron.

Their first task was preparing the cottage in the glen for his mother and Margery. Of course all the grates and fire-irons, pots and pans, locks and hinges, were forged by the old lady in her own cavern, and it was wonderful how clever she was at carpentering too.

"I think your mother may move in to-morrow," she observed, as they were giving a last look round to see that all was right.

"It's as complete as can be," replied Johnny, glancing at the china in the cupboard and the clock against the wall. "There's only one thing I shall miss."

"And what is that?" asked the Money-woman.

"Oh, it's only our old see-saw."

"Go and look out of your bedroom window," said the Money-woman.

And behold, there was the see-saw on which he had played so often, balanced across its original old stump of tree, and looking as natural as possible. How the Money-woman ever got it there, or how she knew that he cared about it, remains a mystery to this day. But the very next evening Johnny and Margery had such a grand game of play on it that they quite lost count of how many times they had each fallen off, and at last became so weak with laughing, that they could neither swing it up nor down, and so had to give up and go in.

They lived very happily in their new house, and Johnny soon became a very useful servant to the Money-woman, and was often allowed to travel to distant lands on her errands. When he grew up he married Margery, and they had a merry family of children, who were as fond of the see-saw as their father and mother had been. Johnny must have picked up some odd names in his journeyings to foreign lands, for his eldest boy and girl were called Gottlieb and Nimmy. Nimmy stayed at home with her mother and grandmother, and a good useful little maiden she was ; but Gottlieb went down to help his father in the Money-woman's cave. At first he only made silver pennies, and such small coin, at tiny fires of his own ; so that when the other children saw a little bit of burning wood or coal drop out of the fireplace at home, and blaze for a minute on the hearth below, they called it "Gottlieb's fire," until "Gottlieb's fires" became quite a saying in the family.

The Money-woman and Johnny and Gottlieb are still at work, and there is not much likelihood at present of their having to give up. And if you are careful to spend your money wisely and kindly and liberally, even if you have not found them at it yet, some day you will find that the good Money-woman's fingers, or perhaps little Gottlieb's instead of hers, have been busy in your purse, secretly adding to your store when you least expected it. So a long life to them all and a busy one, and may their fires never burn dim !

OSMOND AND ALRED LANDING ON THE ICEBERG.

X.—BAA, BAA, BLACK SHEEP.

" Baa, baa, black sheep, have you any wool?
Yes, massa, plenty, three bags full.
One for my master, one for my dame,
And one for the little boy that lives in the lane."

IN a grass-grown and almost deserted lane there once lived a little boy, who had made there for himself a sort of hut or hole to live in. He had scooped away the earth in the high overhanging bank so as to make a little cave, and had fenced the front of it with sticks and branches, leaving only a low doorway through which to creep in and out. It was indeed not much bigger than a dog-kennel, but it was the best he could make, and the little boy had no one to help him to make anything better. He had no friends, nobody to love or to care for him. He was alone all day, and when he came home tired to his cave at night, there was nobody there to welcome him. The first thing that he could remember was being brought up by a black sheep that belonged to the flock of the Squire through whose land the lane ran. As soon as he could run about he was expected to do all sorts of odd jobs and messages, and the Squire gave him in return crusts ot bread and other scraps from his kitchen, and now and then an old worn-out garment that had belonged to his own little boy. It was not a very happy life for the poor boy, for he was of a loving and sociable nature, and it grieved him when the other boys refused to play with him, and looked down on him because he had no home and no friends and even no name, for he was never called anything except "The little boy that lives in the lane."

One fine spring day, as the little boy was passing a pond that lay near his lane, he saw a number of other boys sailing little boats in the water, pushing them out with sticks, blowing at their sails to make them start, and running shouting round to receive them on the other side. The little boy stopped to watch the fun, and thought how nice it would be if he were a wee wee little fellow, no bigger than a fly, and could go sailing about in one of those boats. Then he thought he would join the game, and began shouting and running with the rest. But one of them stopped and said, "We don't want you; where is your boat? Nobody must come and play with us unless he brings a boat."

"But I haven't got a boat," said the little boy.

"Then ask your daddy to get you one."

"But I have no daddy to ask," replied the little boy. "Please let me stay; I won't touch your boats; I will only look."

"We can't play with beggar-boys," said another boy. "You should get your shirt mended, you are not fit to be with us."

For the poor little boy had nothing on but a ragged little

shirt, and a pair of trousers that were much too short for him. "I have nobody to mend my shirt for me," he said, "and I have not got another."

"Go to its friend, the black sheep, then," said a boy, "and get her to make it one of her own black wool." .

"What! is that our little boy that lives in the lane?" exclaimed the Squire's son, who just then came up with a new boat in his hand, gay with flags and streamers. "What are you doing here, boy? idling away your time as usual? Go and pick up a bundle of dry sticks if you have nothing else to do."

And the poor little boy turned away from the pond, and walked slowly towards the wood, and the little fleet set off on its voyage again.

The black sheep, whom the others had called the little nameless boy's friend, was meantime feeding with the rest of the flock on the downs. The shepherd boy and his dog were both lying asleep, for it was very seldom that any one came by to disturb the sheep. A traveller, however, did come across the downs that afternoon, and made straight for the sheep as soon as he saw them. He was but a youth, although taller and stronger than many a full-grown man, for his face was still smooth and boyish. His shoes were dusty and worn, as though he had travelled far; nevertheless he tramped manfully on until he came up to the nearest black sheep.

"Baa, baa, black sheep, have you any wool?" he asked.

"Baa-a-a!" replied the sheep, and turned round to run

away. The traveller thereupon went to another black sheep and asked the same question. But he got no answer at all ; the sheep looked at him stupidly for a moment, and then went on nibbling at the grass. The stranger would not give up, however, and turned to the next black sheep, which happened to be the one who was such a good friend to the little boy that lived in the lane. Now this one was not a common sheep at all. The fairies had taken a fancy to it when it was a lamb, because it was quite black all over, and was so frisky and playful: and they had made it join their sports when they came out to dance by moonlight on the green, and had played hide and seek in its woolly coat, and ridden it in their fairy rings, and decked it with crystals made from moonbeams, which are fairies' diamonds. In return, they had given it the power of speech, and many other fairy gifts. So when the traveller came to it and said,

> " Baa, baa, black sheep, have you any wool ?"

the sheep answered at once,

> " Yes, massa, plenty, three bags full.
>   One for my master, one for my dame,
>   And one for the little boy that lives in the lane."

Then the traveller said again,

> " Where is the little boy, and what is his name ?
>   Tell me, tell me, black sheep, and whence 'tis he came."

> " He wanders in the woods here, he has no name,
>   And no one in the country knows from whence he came,"

replied the black sheep.

"Then it must be he whom I have travelled so far to find,"

said the youth, "and you are Babaa the sheep who brought him up and were so kind to him."

"Yes I did," said Babaa, for that was the name that the fairies had given her; "but what do you know about us?"

"Come down into this hollow where we shall not be disturbed," said the stranger, "for I have much to say to you."

And he sat down there, and he and the black sheep talked together for a long time, but so low that nobody but a fairy could have heard what they were saying; and then the traveller got up and went towards the lane.

The little boy had picked up a bundle of sticks, as he was bidden, and carried it to the Squire's house, where the cook gave him his plateful of scraps. But as he came away from the back-door he saw the Squire's little son going in at the front with his boat in his arms. And his mother came out to meet him, and kissed him, and told him to come in to supper, for he must be hungry, and asked whether he was sure his feet were not wet: and the Squire called out of the window to know how the boat had sailed. And the boy answered merrily, and went into the house with his arm thrown round his mother. When the little boy that lived in the lane saw all this, and thought how he had nobody at home to care for him or for him to care for, he felt as if his heart would burst; and presently he could bear it no longer, but sat down under the hedge and cried heartily. He was crying so that he did not see the traveller coming until he put his hand on his shoulder and said—

"What is the matter, my child ? why are you crying ?"

"Because I have nobody belonging to me," said the little boy, "nobody to care for."

"Take me, then," said the stranger, kindly. "Night is coming on and I have nowhere to go to : will you take me home ?"

"Oh yes !" cried the little boy, jumping up. But when he saw the handsome, well-dressed stranger, he hesitated. "At least, I have no real home," he said. "I made my little house myself, but the boys laugh at it and call it a rat-hole. It is not so bad, though, when once you are inside : only you are so big, I don't know whether you can get in."

"Oh, I will get in," said the stranger. And so he did, somehow, and declared he was very comfortable, although he could not possibly have sat upright if he had wanted ever so much. The little boy made haste and brought out all his scraps, giving much the largest half to his guest. But somehow he enjoyed that half supper better than he had ever done a whole one.

When they had finished, the stranger said, "Come and sit here by me, my little boy ; I want to have a talk with you. Do you know it is not really true that you have no one belonging to you, for I am your own brother, and have come all this way to look for you ?"

The little boy was so much astonished that he could hardly believe it, and sat gazing at his new brother from under his bushy locks of hair. At last he said, " My very own brother ' and I thought I had no brother ! Have you got a name ?"

"Yes, my name is Osmond."

"And have I got a name too?"

"Yes, dear little brother, your name is Alred."

"Osmond—Alred; what beautiful names," cried the little boy, who had always been specially vexed at not having any name like other boys.

"And you are beautiful too," he added, peeping up at his brother again. "But where have you been all this long time?"

"In a country that is a great way off, where you were born," said Osmond; "I will tell you about it. When you were a baby we lived there with our father and mother and sister, and were as happy as happy could be. But there came a fierce dragon into the land, and lurked in caves and waste places, and killed all the passers-by. Our father was the bravest knight in the kingdom, and he went out and slew the dragon, and every one rejoiced. But another dragon, a very terrible one, heard of it, and determined to punish our father. He is called the Dragon of the Dark Mist, because wherever he goes he is folded in a thick mist so that nobody can see him coming. He made agreement with a whirlwind to help him, and he bore him over land and sea until he came swooping down over our house, and caught up my father and mother and sister, and you too, into the dark mist and fled away. Only I was left, for I was out in the forest practising with my bow and arrow, and did not know what the strange mist meant which I saw come down over our house. When the king heard what had happened, he took me into the palace and brought me up and was very kind to me.   But I could never be contented until I had found out what was become of you and the others. So as soon as I was old enough to go, the good king gave me money for the undertaking, and let me wander forth in search of our father and mother."

"You have not found them though?" inquired Alred.

"Not yet," said Osmond.   "I went first to Far-seer the hermit, who lives on the top of Eagle's-eye crag, and who knows more secrets than any other man in the world.   He told me that our father and mother and sister lie sleeping in the far-off Dragon Caves, where the Dragon of the Dark Mist dwells unseen, and whose entrance is guarded by an ever-blowing whirlwind from foot of man or beast.   But you, he said, were not there, for the dragon had dropped you to earth as he whirled along."

On hearing this, Alred could not help glancing down at himself, as if to see whether any of his limbs showed signs of ever having been broken.

"The hermit said that you were uninjured," continued Osmond, "for you fell into the midst of a fairy ring, and those who do so are never hurt.   A black sheep that was the fairies' friend had found you there, he said, and had tended and brought you up until now you had grown to be a sturdy boy. So I determined to look first for my little brother, that we might go together in search of the Dragon Caves."

"That was good of you," said Alred, returning Osmond's caress.   "But how did you know Babaa from all the other black sheep?"

"I went to every black sheep I saw until I came to her," said Osmond. "She told me all she knew about you, and we are to see her again to-morrow morning, for she has promised to ask the fairies whether they know the way to the Dragon Caves."

"And shall we start to-morrow?" said Alred.

"Yes."

"And you will never go away and leave me any more?"

"No, never."

Little Alred slept very happily by his brother's side, and his first thought, when he woke the next morning, was to see whether he was still there. Yes, there he lay, the kind, big, new elder brother. As if to make sure to himself that it was he, Alred whispered, softly, "Brother Osmond."

"Yes, brother Alred," said Osmond opening his eyes.

"Oh! I did not mean to wake you," said Alred, "only it is so pleasant to have somebody to love and to speak to."

Osmond laughed and gave him a hug, and said they would go and find Babaa on the down.

As he trotted along by his brother's side Alred wished very much to meet some of the boys who would not play with him yesterday. But it was so early that nobody was astir, not even the shepherd.

"Well, good Babaa, have you anything to tell us," said Osmond, as they came up to her.

"Not so much as I should wish," replied Babaa. "The fairies do not know the way to the Dragon Caves, for they say that they are hidden in the land of mist and fog; but they know of some one who does, and that is the Great White She-Bear.   But she lives amid icebergs and everlasting snows close to the North Pole, and they who would go to her must have warm desires and ardent wills indeed, to withstand the cold of her halls of ice."

" We will go there if she can tell us the way to the Dragon Caves," said Osmond.   " But how shall we reach her ?"

" You must travel ever northward," replied Babaa, " until you come to the city that stands on the shores of the Frozen Sea.   There you must buy a sealskin boat, and row still northward until you find the great ice-cavern and the White Bear sitting within, and her companions round her.   But the king of the country through which you pass is cruel and covetous, and if he hears where you are going he will lay a tribute on you of a thousand crowns, and cast you into prison because you cannot pay it him.   Therefore, the fairies say, you must be on your guard as you journey through his land."

Osmond thanked her, but said that he hoped the king would hardly notice two such insignificant travellers.   " And how shall we secure the friendship of the Great White Bear," he added, " when we get to her ?"

" I have thought of that," said Babaa, looking up with her wise yellow eyes.   " See, when I was shorn the other day I put aside a bag of my wool to make a warm jacket for my little boy in the lane ; but now you shall take it with you to present to the White Bear.   She will be so pleased with its warmth and its colour that she will grant you whatever you ask."

The brothers took it and thanked her, and the sheep said to Alred, "You will not forget your old Babaa, will you ?"

" Oh no," said Alred.   " Shan't we go now, brother ?"

And they bade her good-bye, and started.

They stopped in the first town that they came to, to buy Alred a suit of clothes ; and then they travelled hand-in-hand ever northward, through the shady woods and along the green lanes, across the commons and over the downs. And the country grew bleaker and wilder, and the sky greyer and colder, as they went on and on until they entered the kingdom that bordered on the Frozen Sea. They soon found out when they had crossed the border, for people began to look coldly at them, and to ask why they came and what their business was. They kept to the lanes and fields as much as they could, but they were forced to go into the villages to buy food, and sometimes to ask their way.

One day they had turned aside from the road and sat down by a spring to eat their dinner, and Alred climbed up an ash-tree to see whether the town to which they were going was yet in sight. He was just coming down when he heard voices below, and saw two men meeting under the tree.

" Whither away ?" said one.

" I am after two young rogues," replied the other, " who are travelling through the country and won't tell their business, nor have they paid tribute to the king. They passed along here only half an hour ago, so I shall soon catch them and clap them into prison unless they can pay the thousand crowns.   You have not, met them, have you ? a tall youth, and a stout, lusty boy with him ?"

"Not that I remember ; but if I do I will be sure to lay hold of them," was the reply.   And then the men went on their way.

"We must turn back to some out-of-the-way place until this hunt for us is over," said Osmond, "and then disguise ourselves and work our way up again by some other road."

So back they turned, and Alred was quite consoled when he heard Osmond's plan for enabling them to pass unquestioned. He made a quantity of little wooden lambs, putting a little bit of the black sheep's wool on each, and then he soiled his own clothes on purpose, and turned his fur cap inside out, while Alred put on his old ragged shirt over his other clothes. Thus dressed, they sallied forth as travelling toy-merchants, Alred carrying a tray with all the little lambs spread out on it, and whenever they passed through a town or village, Osmond cried—

> " Young lambs to sell ! young lambs to sell !
> If I had as much money as I could tell,
> I never would cry, Young lambs to sell !"

Black lambs ! Nobody had ever seen such toys before, and every little boy and girl wanted to have one. It was great fun, and nobody thought of asking them what was their business now, and Osmond's purse grew quite heavy again. At last, when there was only one lamb left, they reached the top of a high hill, and behold there lay the Frozen Sea before them, and on its shore stood the city to which they must go.

Osmond brushed his clothes and turned his cap right side out again, and Alred took off his ragged shirt, and they went down into the city and bought the best sealskin boat that they could find. The winds were still and the sea calm, so they took their boat to the water's edge and launched forth at once. Osmond took the oars and Alred steered, and away they went ever northward across the cold grey waters.

"Brother," said Alred by-and-by, "I see such a big iceberg straight in front of us, and it has a great hole in it like the mouth of a cave."

"It is a cave, too," said Osmond; "I do believe we have reached the end of our voyage. Let us land and explore."

They moored the boat to a block of ice, and stepped on to the iceberg, making straight for the cave's mouth. Huge icicles as big as pine-tree stems hung from it like a portcullis ready to drop on them, and the ice within was of the loveliest emerald green, and the floor of beaten snow. At the entrance sat a little fox all in thick white fur, with sharp little eyes and a bushy white tail. He started up and pricked up his ears when he saw Osmond and Alred, and ran forward and then back towards the cave again, as if inviting them to come in. They followed their little guide, and were immediately joined by another and another white fox, and then another and another, until thirty little white foxes were trotting noiselessly beside them upon the smooth snow-floor. On they went along the great green-lit tunnel of ice, until it seemed as if they must be coming to the very middle of the iceberg, when their way was suddenly stopped by a massive block of ice. The thirty foxes all gave a run and jump, and came bang against it with their tails, and the ice-door swung silently open, and lo! they stood in the hall of the Great White She-Bear. What a bear it was! If you had set a four-storied house down beside her, she could easily have looked down the chimneys without getting up, or even raising her head. Her back was like the side of a snow-mountain, and her legs were like martello towers, only longer and larger. The hall was of the size it ought to be for such an inhabitant. There were no windows in it, but the light shone calm and grey through the mighty ice-walls and roof. Round the hall sat seven-and-twenty smaller bears, who formed the Great Bear's court. There they sat night and day, winter and summer. Now and then one of them grew hungry, or wanted to see how his wife and children were getting on, and he would get up and steal slowly out, returning silently to his place after a time. The Great Bear herself never was hungry except once in two or three years but then when she ate, she did eat! She would eat a whale at one sitting, with several dozen of smaller fish at the same time by way of sauce.

She slowly turned her great head as the brothers entered, and looking at them with her large sleepy eyes she said, " Youths, disclose your purpose."

Her voice was like a stormy gust of wind losing itself in a mountain gully ; and when she spoke the twenty-seven smaller bears raised themselves and turned their heads exactly as she had done.

" O Great White Bear," said Osmond, kneeling on one knee

before her, " we are two brothers who are seeking the way to the Caves of the Dragon of the Dark Mist, and we have been told that none but your highness (he might well call her that, for he could hardly see her face, it was so high) can tell us the road. And so we have ventured to come to your domain, and to bring with us this little offering."

As he said this, Alred stepped forward and opened the bag of black wool. The Great Bear was delighted with it, it was so warm and so fine, and above all so black ; for everything is white at the North Pole, and one's eyes get so tired of it that a little black is really quite refreshing. The Great She-Bear tore off a little bit of the wool and handed it round for her twenty-seven councillors to look at, and they all said, " What a lovely colour ! What a cheering tint !" Then she made a sort of mat of it for her right fore-paw to rest upon, and said to Osmond, " Proceed."

Osmond then told her about his father having killed the dragon, and how the other dragon had carried them off, and begged her to tell them how to find the Dragon Caves, and what to do when they had found them. But when he got as far as that, the She-Bear raised her right paw and said, " Pause, youth ; I must meditate."

Then she folded her fore-paws and shut her eyes, and the seven-and-twenty smaller bears all round the hall did the same, while Osmond and Alred drew back quietly and waited.

They were getting very tired of waiting at the end of half an hour, when one of the little white foxes popped in his head and winked and nodded to them to come out with him. Accordingly they followed him into a smaller ice-hall, where they found a feast of frozen fish and other Arctic dainties spread out for them, to which they were well pleased to sit down, for the cold air had given them an appetite. While they ate, the thirty foxes danced an Arctic reel for their amusement, which presently changed into a game of leap-frog, and Osmond and Alred joined in it and had great fun.

The White Bear's meditation lasted for three days, after which she sent for the brothers and said, in her deep gusty voice, that always sounded a long way off, " I have considered your case, and have determined to assist you. The Cave of the Dragon of the Dark Mist lies far eastward in the Plains of Barren Limestone, beyond the Flint Mountains. The way thereto is hard, wherefore I have caused this map to be prepared for your guidance. When by its help you reach the cave you will find the entrance thereof guarded by a fierce and unapproachable whirlwind.. Take therefore also this small bottle, which opening, you shall both repeat these words—

' From the silent lair
Of the Great White Bear
Float forth, O Flake,
And stillness make.'

You may then pass unhindered into the caves which you desire to enter."

With that the White She-Bear handed them a map and a bottle with a single snowflake corked up in it, and, heaving a deep sigh, was about to compose herself to rest, when one of the seven-and-twenty bears held up his claw and said, " Dark."

" In the cave," continued another.

" Light," said a third.

" How to get ?" added a fourth.

" True," said the Great White Bear. " I must meditate."

So she meditated for five days more ; and Osmond and Alred spent the time, as before, merrily enough with the white foxes. Indeed, if they had not kept constantly running about, they would have been frozen to the place where they stood, the cold was so great. When the White Bear had summoned them the second time, she said :

" Youths ! The. darkness which surrounds the Dragon of the Dark Mist is so great that neither torch nor taper nor any other light is of the slightest use in his gloomy cavern, except it be a feather from the breast of the Phœnix. My advice to you therefore is to go to him before journeying to the Barren Limestone Plains."

" And how shall we find our way to him, your highness ?" asked Osmond, seeing that the Great Bear was shutting her eyes again.

" You know my grand-uncle," said the Bear, slowly opening them.

" I am afraid we don't," said Osmond.

" Not the Great Bear in the sky just above us ?"

" Oh yes, to be sure we do !" cried both the brothers.

" Good ! He is my grand-uncle," said the Bear. " Keep your backs always turned to him, and walk on until he seems to sink out of sight behind the horizon. Then you will find the Phœnix."

M

"May we say that we come from your highness?" asked Osmond.

"You may," said the White Bear, graciously. "You shall also take him a piece of ice, which will please him so that he will give you all you want."

"But it will melt long and long before we get there," said Alred.

The Great She-Bear took no notice of this speech, but the other bears all shook their heads reprovingly. Then they got up and fetched a small slab of ice from a spot to which she pointed, and laid it at her feet, forming in a ring round it with all their fore-paws held up in the air. In this position they chanted in their deep, gruff voices, and as slowly as if there had been a full stop after each word—

"Melt . Not . Slice .
Of . Arc . tic . Ice."

This they repeated three times, and then went back to their places. Thereupon the little foxes ran in and briskly tied up the ice into a tidy parcel in a large sheet of goldbeaters' skin and presented it to Osmond.

He and Alred began to thank the Great White Bear, but she interrupted them, saying, "Peace, youths! Having got all you want, depart."

"I should like to ask one thing more, if you don't mind," said Osmond. "When we have got into the cave, what ought we to do to the Dragon?"

"Do? Nothing," growled the Great White Bear, and rolled herself round with her back to them, and her nose on the patch of black sheep's wool.

So Osmond and Alred went away, out of the great white hall, along the emerald-lighted passage, under the icicle-portcullis, and stepped into their sealskin boat again. The friendly little foxes went with them to the water's edge, and waved a farewell with their bushy white tails, and scampered home again. The Great White She-Bear was so tired with the exertions she had made, that she slept for three years and a half without turning. At the end of that time she roused up and ate five preserved whales, seven walruses, and ninety-four smaller fish, such as sharks and conger-eels; after which she turned her black sheep's wool mat and felt pretty well again.

But the brothers rowed away quickly, glad to escape from that cold, silent hall.

"You were getting so blue and pale there, brother," observed Alred. "If we had stayed much longer I think we should have turned as white as the little foxes. I hope the Phœnix does not live in an iceberg: do you think he does?"

"I should think not," said Osmond, "for if he did, the Great White Bear would hardly have sent him a present of ice. I wonder how long the journey will take us."

They found that the great iceberg had floated so far while they were in it, that although they rowed straight back south again, they landed in quite a different part of the country. This, however, was rather an advantage, for nobody knew them, and so they were not obliged to spend any more time in selling young lambs, but pushed on as fast as they could, taking care to keep the White Bear's great-uncle at their backs. Soon they left behind the frost and snow, and the country became greener. Instead of dark pine woods they passed through oak forests, then orchards and chestnut groves, then olive yards. Still they journeyed south: aloes and prickly-pears grew by the wayside, and the banks of the streams were fringed with oleanders. Instead of the silence of the Arctic regions, birds sang and insects chirped and whizzed and hummed all round them. Then the grass became scorched and brown from the heat of the sun, and the only trees that they could see were acacias and palms. How refreshing a nibble at that lump of ice would have been ! It was very tempting, but they would not touch it, and tramped manfully on over the hot dry sand.

"I cannot see the Great Bear in the sky to-night," observed Osmond, as they halted to rest in a clump of palms that grew beside a spring. "He seems to have quite sunk below the horizon now."

"Oh, I am so glad !" cried Alred. "Then we must get to the Phœnix soon."

Long before sunrise the next morning they were on their way again, looking out eagerly for any signs of the Phœnix. For some hours they saw nothing ; but towards noon, when they were longing for a little shade from the burning rays of the sun, they beheld a single palm-tree in the distance. It was the strangest tree they had ever seen, for the stem seemed to be made of a red-hot shaft of molten ore, and instead of feathery palm leaves, there rose from it an ever-flowing fiery fountain that always faded into nothing when it had fallen a few feet, and yet was always springing afresh. And lo! in the midst of this fire-palm sat the Phœnix, glowing in the intense heat as though an inward fire were burning under his own plumage. He looked so grand and terrible all alone there, that the boys paused, half fearing to advance.

He did not feel grand and terrible, however, the lonely Phœnix. He felt sad and deserted, for he longed for a companion, and he had no friends nor relations, nor even visiting acquaintances, for neither beast nor bird could bear to linger in that scorching air. Once, a long time ago, three birds had tried it; they had come and made their home on a large stone that lay near the foot of the fiery palm. But the heat was so great that they could not stay, and one by one they flew away again. The Phœnix was sorry, and pitied the stone, and wondered whether it felt as lonely as he did. And he made this little song about the three birds, and sang it over and over to himself:

> "Three little birds sat on a stone,
> Two flew away and then there was one.
> One flew away and then there was none,
> And so the poor stone was left all alone."

When the Phœnix saw Osmond and Alred, he stopped short in his song, and said, "Welcome fair youths. What brings you to my lonely land, untrodden by the foot of man?"

"O great Phœnix, we are come to beg a favour of you," replied Osmond, "and we bring this piece of ice as a present from the Great White Bear who lives in the Frozen Sea."

And he stood on tiptoe to reach it up, shading his face from the heat as he did so.

The Phœnix was delighted with the gift, and laid it close to his heart, where he might feel its refreshing coolness. For you know this was a charmed pieco of ice, and it neither melted in the flames nor lost any of its cold. Then the Phœnix asked the brothers again what they wanted, and they told him of the Dragon Caves to which they were going, and how they had visited the Great White Bear in her iceberg hall, and that she had told them that nothing but a feather from the breast of the Phœnix could serve to light them on their dangerous adventure. The Phœnix listened, gazing at them with his bright eyes, and when they had finished he plucked the largest feather from his breast and gave it to Osmond, saying, "I rejoice to be able to help you; take it, and may you succeed in all that you wish to do!"

When Osmond saw that he was so friendly, he ventured to ask him the same question that he had asked of the Bear: "What ought we to do to the Dragon when we get into the cave?"

"It is of no use trying to fight him," replied the Phœnix, "for neither blow nor thrust can wound him, unless, indeed, you could succeed in striking him with the feather. But above all, do not on any account let go the feather. As long as you hold it fast, you are the Dragon's master, and he cannot hurt you."

"But only one of us can hold it," said Osmond.

"Let the other hold closely to the one who has it," said the Phœnix.

The brothers thanked him, and were going, when he called them back. "I wish you could send me word how you have prospered," he said. "I wonder whether the Salamander is still there, whom the Dragon took prisoner and shut up in a mass of igneous limestone. If you should find him, send him to me to tell me how you have sped. And say to him from me, that if he will come and live with me he shall find a warm welcome here, and a safe retreat."

The boys promised, and went on their way across the burning desert sands. The Phœnix had all but called them back again to ask them whether they had met three birds anywhere in the neighbourhood, only he remembered that they had flown away years ago. So instead of calling them he began again his mournful song of

"Three little birds sat upon a stone."

"We have reached it at last! here is the cave at last!" exclaimed Osmond and Alred, as they stood on the edge of a dark chasm in the midst of a barren plain. They had been travelling now for more than two years altogether; the map which had guided them was falling to pieces with constant use; their clothes were worn and ragged, and their faces brown with exposure; but they were as eager to find their father and mother as on the day they had started; and they had not lingered even for a day in any of the strange towns or fair gardens through which they had passed.

"But how desolate it is here! this is worse than the Frozen Sea," said Alred, looking round him. There was not a tree nor a blade of grass to be seen. In the distance were the dark Flint Mountains that they had crossed, and before them lay the Barren Limestone Plain, with great rocks and boulders tumbled upon it, as if a gang of giant carters had upset waggon-loads of them all about. A dull, heavy mist hung over the place, and not a breath of air was stirring, except in the mouth of the cave. There, indeed, it was all commotion, and as Osmond and Alred came nearer to the hole and looked down, their caps were torn off and sucked down, and themselves nearly carried off their legs by the violence of the Whirlwind. They could just see him in the darkness, spinning round and round on one leg, with flying garments and streaming hair. "Away! away! away!" shrieked the Whirlwind, catching wildly at their feet. "I will tear you to pieces—I will whirl you to atoms—I will—ah ah a——ee!"

For the brothers speedily let out the bottled snow-flake, repeating together—

> " From the Arctic lair
> Of the Great White Bear
> Float forth, O Flake,
> And stillness make."

The snow-flake floated calmly into the midst of the eddy, and the Whirlwind collapsed like a balloon that has burst, and then fled howling up into the air, tearing and scattering the mists on his way.

There was nothing now to prevent their entering, and Osmond and Alred began to clamber carefully down the steep sides into the darkness, Osmond holding up the Phœnix-feather in one hand, and grasping Alred's hand firmly with the other. The darkness became so thick that they could hardly breathe ; but the darker it grew the brighter shone the Feather, until a stream of light seemed to come out from every point. At last they felt the ground more level under their feet, and looked eagerly about for the Dragon. Nothing living was to be seen through the dark mist-clouds, and they groped their way towards what seemed to be the entrance to an inner cavern.

"Halloa ! stop him, he looks as if he were bent on mischief !" cried Alred, darting forward at a scorpion that was running past them into that inner cave. The ugly little black reptile brandished its tail at them, but they had been too quick for it, and stood between it and the cave, holding out the Phœnix-feather. The scorpion shrank back from it, and hunched up its back ; and behold while they watched it grew and grew and grew, until it glared at them with great eyes, and snapped at them with huge claws, and writhed its black coils through the whole length of the cavern, and they saw that it was none other than the Dragon of the Dark Mist himself. "Sz—sz—sz—sz—" hissed the Dragon, louder and louder, until it was vain to attempt to speak, or even shout to one another. The noise and rolling darkness were very confusing, and in the midst of it all began a match between the Dragon and the brothers. He made dashes at them, trying to enter the cave, or to separate them from one another, taking care, however, not to come near enough to be touched by the shining Feather.

"He may keep on at this game until we are both tired out," thought Osmond. "I must try and put a stop to it if possible." And he made a rush at the Dragon, hoping to reach him before he was aware.

But the Dragon drew back too quickly, and seeing the entrance left for a moment unguarded, he in his turn made a rush to get by.

"Oh, he'll be in!" screamed Alred, forgetting that he could not be heard. He had made up his mind that his father and mother and sister must be in that inner cave, and that the Dragon wanted to get in first in order to kill them or to carry them off. In his eagerness to stop him, he let go Osmond's hand and darted back. Osmond, dismayed at seeing his brother unprotected, bounded after; and the Dragon, whom they had startled out of a sound sleep by their entrance, bewildered with the rapidity of their movements and the flashing of the unaccustomed light, instead of seizing Alred as he intended, came bounce up against Osmond, Phœnix-feather and all, and laid him flat on the ground.

Whizz—bang! The dragon had caught fire from the feather, and with a loud report he flared up and was gone, all except a volume of very ill-smelling smoke that he left behind him, which rolled slowly away into the darkest corners of the cavern.

The cavern shook so with the shock of the Dragon's explosion that Alred found himself lying on his back too. The brothers were soon on their feet again; and after looking all about very carefully to make quite sure that the Dragon had gone off in the explosion, they went into that inner cavern at whose entrance they had fought so long. They had not gone far before they came upon three sleepers lying in a low niche in the rock, with a dark mist brooding over them. To Alred of course they were strangers, but Osmond cried out at once that here were the father and mother and sister whom they had come to seek. Alred threw himself upon them, but neither calling nor caress could rouse them, until Osmond touched them with the shining feather. Then the dark mist shrivelled away, the sleepers opened their eyes, and there was such a joyful greeting, and embracing, and explaining, as at once made up to the boys for all their toilsome wanderings.

No one had any wish to linger in the cave, and they soon began to work their way out, lit by the Phœnix-feather. As they passed by a great rock that seemed newly split, Alred saw a creature on it which reminded him so strongly of the Dragon's scorpion-disguise that he pointed at it, exclaiming in a whisper, "Dragon!"

"I am not a dragon," said the little beast, indignantly. "I am the Salamander. Do give me a touch with that light of yours, for I am nearly dead for want of fire."

The brothers begged its pardon, and gave it the message sent by the Phœnix, asking it at the same time to report to him how well they had succeeded. To this the Salamander readily agreed, and set off at once ; and as he has never been seen again, it is to be hoped that he is still the friend and companion of the Phœnix in his hot, lonely desert.

As for the Great White She-Bear, Osmond and Alred sent

no message to her. Indeed she was still fast asleep, and would not have been at all pleased at any interruption. However, a white ptarmigan that happened to meet Osmond and Alred the following winter brought the news of their good success to the little foxes; and they brandished their bushy tails and danced for joy until they nearly turned brown again with the exercise.

When they had once left the Limestone Plain and the Flint Mountains behind them, what a pleasant journey home that happy family had! Anxious as they were to get home, they went out of their way when they came near the place where Alred had once lived, for the sake of finding Babaa, and bringing her away with them if possible. They found the farmer and his wife willing enough to part with her, for they hardly liked having on the farm a sheep that could talk, and that insisted too on always having a third of her own wool to do what she liked with. She had two bagfuls waiting for Alred when they arrived, and right well pleased she was when they asked her to come and live with them. When the fairies found that she was going, they came too, which was a capital thing for the new pastures, for there is nothing like a troop of fairies for keeping the grass green and fine.

There was only one other place at which the happy party had to stop, and that was at the palace of the good king who had taken such care of Osmond; and then they went straight to their own home.

It was Alred who took Babaa out to her meadows the first time.

"Do you think you shall like them, good Babaa?" he said. "I do hope you will: and to-morrow, father says he will get you some sheep to be your companions, for living all alone is not the way to be happy, as I found when I was a little boy and lived in the lane. I will come back again by-and-by, but I must run in now lest it should be breakfast time, and for fear my father and mother should be waiting for me, and my sister should come down the terrace to look for me, and Osmond should shout from the hall-window for me—Oh, it is all so pleasant! Do you know, Babaa, I think there is only one thing in the world that comes up to being loved, and that is, loving."

And home ran the happy Alred, gathering a handful of roses for his mother and sister as he went.

XI.—BYE, BABY BUNTING.

" Bye, Baby Bunting,
 Father's gone a-hunting,
 Mother's gone a-milking,
 Sister's gone a-silking,
Brother's gone to buy a skin,
To wrap the Baby Bunting in."

BABY BUNTING was the youngest child of Captain Bunting, a brave old sailor, who was the owner of a ship in which he went fighting or trading according as he was wanted. Soon after Baby Bunting was born, Captain Bunting went on a trading trip, in which he was very successful. He was coming home well laden, and with heaps of presents for his wife and children left on shore, when one gusty morning he saw one poor vessel attacked by two great pirate ships. "Hulloh! that's not fair!" said Captain Bunting, and up he sailed with all speed, and helped the vessel to fight the two pirates. A hard fight they had of it ; however, they beat them at last, and made the pirates prisoners on board their own ships. Now, the ship that Captain Bunting had saved was a royal ship, although not of his own country, and it had the King himself on board. As soon as the fight was over, the King sent for Captain Bunting into his own cabin, and thanked him for his help. "Keep close to my vessel," said the King,

BYE, BABY BUNTING.

"and sail home with me to my own land, and I will reward you richly for saving me and my crew."

So Captain Bunting in his merchant ship sailed alongside of the King's vessel. But the wind rose higher and higher, and tossed the curling waves until they dashed right over the decks of the ships. The King's ship had enough to do to look after the two pirate ships that it had in tow; and in that stormy night Captain Bunting lost his rudder, and was driven by the gale far far away from the other ships and from the course in which they were sailing. His ship had been a good deal battered in the fight with the pirates, and she sprang a leak and filled so fast with water, that when morning came she was all but sinking, and they gave themselves up for lost. But when they looked round, behold there were the cliffs of their own shore, and the revenue cutter coming with all sails set to them, to see that they were not smugglers. They had only just time to scramble on board the cutter, when down went the ship like a stone, and all the rich merchandise in her. Poor Captain Bunting and his crew were put on shore with hardly so much as a whole suit of clothes between them. As for the Captain's presents, they had gone to the young oysters and starfishes; but his wife and children did not care for that, when they got him safely home again.

He wrote a letter to the King whose life he had saved, telling him all that had happened. And after he had posted it, he waited day after day, and week after week, but no answer came. At last he said to his wife, "I see the King has forgotten me. He was a very young man, and he looked anxious, and as if his head were full of other things. Never mind, we will do the best we can for ourselves." The King had not forgotten him, however. As soon as he reached land, he made inquiry for him among the captains of all the ships that he could hear of, but of course Captain Bunting was not among them. And his letter never reached the King. It was put into the King's postbag all right enough, but the King's postbag, being a royal one, was not only made of leather like a common postbag, but it was lined with purple silk. It would have been much better for Captain Bunting if they had not lined it so smartly, for the lining came unstitched, and his letter slipped down between the lining and the leather, and was not found again for ten years.

Captain Bunting had no money to buy a new ship, so when he gave up waiting for the King's answer, he made up his mind to look about for employment. Some little feeling of pride, however, made him unwilling to take service in his own home, so hearing that there was plenty of work to be got in the next kingdom, he proposed to his wife to go there.

They began by selling the house and furniture. After they had paid the wages of the ship's crew and everything else that was owing, there was just thirty pounds left for Captain Bunting and his family to travel with to a new country and to set up house there.

Captain Bunting's family consisted of Mrs. Bunting his wife, a girl of fourteen, named Nelly, John, a sharp boy of twelve, and Baby Bunting himself, who was only a few months old. Very glad Mrs. Bunting was to get her baby safely to the end of his journey, and into the little inn, where they must wait till they could get a house.

But though there was plenty of work to be had, not a house could they find. Captain Bunting walked all over the place till he could walk no more, and not one empty house did he hear of.

"What is that little house under the hill?" said Captain Bunting to their landlady. "It looks empty."

"Oh, yes, it's empty," said the landlady, "but no one will ever go there, for it is haunted."

"What with?" said the Captain.

The landlady did not know.

"It will do, then," said Captain Bunting. "When people complain of being haunted, it is their own bad consciences that haunt them. An honest heart and a clear conscience need be afraid of nothing—except, perhaps, sea-pirates. So in we go."

And in they went. It was a nice little house, rather dark perhaps at the back from being under the hillside, but they put up Baby Bunting's cradle in the snuggest corner, and made themselves very comfortable. The next day all the people in the place turned out to see what had happened to the family who had dared to sleep in the house under the hill. But nothing had happened, except that Baby Bunting had slept remarkably well, at which the people were very much disappointed.

Captain Bunting soon got a place as under-gamekeeper to a rich squire who was very fond of shooting. John hired himself out as grocer's errand-boy, and Nelly found work at a silk-factory in the town. To be sure, they had never expected to have to work like this, but they did not grumble. They were earning their bread honestly, and that was a great satisfaction to them.

Before long Mrs. Bunting had an offer to go and milk the squire's cows. She very much wished to do it, for they not only promised to pay her money, but to give her a jug of milk every day for Baby Bunting. It would be such a good thing for him, she thought, but how could she leave him all alone? "Even if he sleeps quietly in his cradle, I am afraid he will get so cold in the winter weather," she observed.

"Look here, mother," said John. "I have got to take a parcel of tea to the furrier's this afternoon; suppose I see whether I cannot buy a nice warm rabbit-skin to wrap baby in while you are out milking."

"Yes, do, John," said his mother. "And I daresay your father will be home in time to take baby for me this afternoon."

But the squire had a great shooting party that day, and Captain Bunting was wanted to hunt up the game for the gentlemen to shoot at, for this is what they called sport in that country. So when milking time came Captain Bunting was out hunting, John was gone to buy the skin, Nelly was at the silk factory, and Baby Bunting must be left alone. His mother rocked him in the cradle, and sang to him—

> " Bye, Baby Bunting,
>   Father's gone a-hunting,
>   Mother's gone a-milking,
>   Sister's gone a silking,
> Brother's gone to buy a skin,
> To wrap the Baby Bunting in."

And the moment Baby Bunting shut his eyes his mother ran out at the door and away to her milking as fast as she could go. It seemed to her to take a very long time, and she heartily wished she had never left the baby. She fancied all sorts of things that might have happened to him; but when she unlocked the door and came rushing in, there he lay wide awake in his cradle, as warm and contented as could be. The room, too, she fancied looked particularly clean and tidy, the fire had kept in wonderfully well, and had she really finished that frock that she was making for baby before she went out? She could not remember doing so; but anyhow, it was done. The next day, and the next, the same thing happened. It seemed as if Baby Bunting particularly liked being left alone; and it seemed, too, that he was in the habit of getting out of his cradle and amusing himself by doing all the odd jobs that he could find to do. It was a great puzzle. Captain Bunting and his wife talked it over, and agreed that as long as they were good and honest nothing would hurt them; so they would just be thankful for the help they got, without trying to understand how it came.

Did Baby Bunting really trot about on those little round, soft feet of his, and sweep, and wash, and sew? I will tell you what happened.

The moment that his mother shut the door after her, the first time that she went out to milk, Baby Bunting opened his eyes again. He waited for a minute, thinking she would come back; but when he found that she did not, he made his merry round mouth into a most doleful face, and drew in his breath for such a roar, that if he had made it I am sure his mother would have heard, although she was already nearly half-way to the milking place, and would have gone back to him. But from the darkest side of the room there glided forward a strange little figure, half dwarf, half lady. The body was bent and humped like a dwarf's, but the face was that of a kind and beautiful lady. As soon as little Baby Bunting saw her sweet face bending over him, he forgot the great roar that he was going to make, and held out his little hands to his new friend. And she folded him warmly in her arms, and sang to him the very words that his mother had just sung before she left him alone :

> " Bye, Baby Bunting,
>   Father's gone a-hunting,
>   Mother's gone a-milking,
>   Sister's gone a-silking,
> Brother's gone to buy a skin,
> To wrap the Baby Bunting in."

And she added—

> " But, Baby Bunting, do not cry,
>   Your Frenhina watches nigh."

Baby Bunting had no thought of crying now. He crowed and laughed while Frenhina, with him in one arm, swept the floor and dusted the room. Then she took up the little frock that was lying half made on the table, and sewed away with her white, delicate fingers, still singing the same song of " Bye, Baby Bunting." Her hands went fast enough, but when she walked it seemed to be with difficulty, and almost as though her feet were tied. Her dress was very strange ; it seemed to be made of finely-spun and woven silver ; not bright, glittering silver though, but worn and tarnished, and dulled all over, like silver that is held in steam. This strange visitor remained with Baby Bunting until a step was heard outside, and then she popped him back into his cradle, and glided away just as Mrs. Bunting opened the door.

The next day Baby Bunting kicked with joy as soon as Frenhina appeared, and he would be content to lie for an hour together on her knee while she sewed, and listen to her sweet, sad singing. She came regularly every day as soon as everybody else had gone out of the house ; and Mrs. Bunting, finding that her baby was so well cared for, and her work so well done, would sometimes spend half the day out at her marketing, or anything else that she had to do. And Baby Bunting throve and grew, until he could run about holding by the skirt of the tarnished silver dress, chattering merrily to his strange companion.

One day, when Baby Bunting was nearly three years old, he was playing at putting a wooden spoon to bed in the cradle that was all too small for him to sleep in now, and he began rocking it and singing—

> " Bye, Baby Bunting,
>   Father's gone a-hunting,
>   Mother's gone a-milking,
>   Sister's gone a-silking,
> Brother's gone to buy a skin,
> To wrap the Baby Bunting in."

" Dear me !" cried his mother, "just listen to little Owen ! I do believe he is singing the very song that I sang to him the first day I went milking, two years ago. How can he have remembered it? I don't think I have ever sung it since."

"Owen," said Captain Bunting, "who sings that song to you?"

"Lady," said Baby Bunting, taking up his spoon and kissing it, as Frenhina always did to him.

"Come here, my little boy, and tell me about her," said the Captain. "What is she like?"

Baby thought for a little time, and then said, "Like mother." And he was right, too, for he meant that she was kind to him like his mother.

"Does she come to see you?"

"Course she does," said little Owen, who thought that his father was very stupid to ask such a question.

"And what does she do?"

But Baby Bunting would not tell.

"Does she sing any other songs to you?" said the Captain.

And Baby Bunting began a string of wild scraps of songs, about gold that gleams from rocky seams, and treasure heaps of ore that fill the mighty caverns of the hill, and of dark vaults, the dismal home of the metal-making gnome, of all which they could make neither head nor tail. And John laughed, and called him a little romancer, whereupon Baby Bunting was so indignant, that when they went on to ask the name of his lady, he replied, "S'ant tell." Nor could they get from him a word more about her.

But Frenhina had either heard this conversation, and feared lest they should question little Owen further, and lay wait for her and try to discover her, or else she had an unusual quantity of work to do somewhere else ; certain it is, that from that day she was much less with Baby Bunting. When she did come, she no longer sang to him about the gloomy caverns in the hill, but put her finger on her lip, and glided softly away again as soon as her work was done. Her fairy hands still worked for them every day, though she often now came only when even the baby himself was out of the house. And the boy still throve and grew, until he was no longer Baby Bunting, but schoolboy Owen, a fine, manly little fellow, who never told a lie or hid the truth, and who could not bear to see a child or a beast ill-treated, but would stand up and fight for them like a little lion.

The family of the Buntings had grown so accustomed to the services of their unknown visitor, that they forgot to be curious as to who it could be. Nothing happened to disturb their quiet life in the house under the hill until Owen was nearly ten years old. Then a fever broke out in the day-school which he went to, and little Owen was one of the boys who caught it.

They nursed him, and doctored him, and did all they could for him, but he grew worse and worse, and at last the doctor said that he could do no more, and that little Owen would not recover. The Buntings were in despair. They watched beside him the night after the doctor had given him up, not knowing but that it might be the last that they could do so. But when morning came, Captain Bunting and John and Nelly were so worn out with grief and watching, that they fell fast asleep, and Mrs. Bunting remained sitting by his bedside alone.

The sun had just risen, when there glided suddenly to the other side of the bed a dwarf lady in tarnished silver, who held in her hand what looked like a rough nugget of gold, scooped out into a cup.

" Let him drink, let him drink," whispered the stranger. And the mother, raising her boy's head, poured into his mouth a few drops of sparkling liquid which the cup contained. It seemed to relieve the pain in his head at once, and Owen, after giving a grateful glance to his well-known friend as she laid a cool wet cloth on his forehead, presently closed his eyes and fell fast asleep.

Then the dwarf lady, who had stood watching him anxiously, clasped her hands together and whispered, " He will live !"

And Mrs. Bunting threw her arms round her neck, and thanked her again and again.

" Oh, do not go away," she said, when her visitor moved to go. But the stranger pointed to Captain Bunting, who was beginning to stir, and whispering, " I will come back when you are alone," she disappeared.

When Captain Bunting and Nelly and John saw the change that had come over Owen, they nearly woke him in their delight. But Mrs. Bunting soon sent them all out, saying that Owen must be kept very quiet. Then the stranger came gliding back again, and persuaded Mrs. Bunting to sleep a little too, while she sat and watched by Owen as she had so often done before.

Under Frenhina's care and medicine little Owen got better very quickly, and soon only required feeding up to make him strong enough to get up again.

"Yours is wonderful medicine," said Mrs. Bunting once, as she held in her hand Frenhina's strange nugget-cup. "What is it?"

"It is a mineral that I get in the hill," replied Frenhina. "I knew it had wonderful powers; but as long as the doctor was attending Owen, I thought he would know what was best to give him."

"But after he had given him up, why did you not come to us all that long night?" said Mrs. Bunting. "Though now I think of it, you never do come in the night."

"I cannot," said the dwarf. "From sunset to sunrise I must be at my work in the caverns of the hill."

"In the hill!" exclaimed Mrs. Bunting. "What do you work at there?"

"I serve the King of the Mines—the metal-maker. He lives in the heart of the mountain, and there he is making great treasures under the earth, of gold and silver, and lead and copper, and all manner of metals. And he has made me his slave, so that I must work for him as long as I live."

"You do not look as if you had been born a slave," said Mrs. Bunting.

Frenhina smiled. "I was born a Queen," she said; "and when I was quite a girl I met the King of this country, and we loved one another, and agreed to marry. But I was an orphan, and my guardians wished me to marry another king whom I did not like at all. I knew that I could have my own way if I only waited until I was of age, but I was impatient and would not wait. I sought for secret ways to get away without my guardian's knowledge, and the King of the Mines heard of it, and he came and offered to bring me safely into this country if I would in return grant him one request. I promised, and he brought me here; but his request was that I would be his queen, and reign here in the mine with him. I refused indignantly, and he thereupon made me his slave. He would have had no power over me, if I had not been doing wrong; but as it was I had no means to stand against him, and here I have been ever since, repenting of my hasty journey and still more hasty promise."

A movement from Owen made them look round, but he seemed to be settling to sleep again. Mrs. Bunting glanced at the dwarfish figure beside her, and wondered that a king should choose so deformed a bride. But then to be sure she was very gentle and lovable.

"Why cannot you escape from the mine?" she asked. "Our door is open, what is there to stop you?"

Frenhina lifted her long skirt of tarnished silver, and pointed to a chain of the finest possible silver wire that was bound round her ankles. "This is as far as my chain will let me go," she said. "And I have been so careful to keep my visits secret, because if the King of the Mines should by any chance hear that I come here, I know he would block up my passage with great rocks, and then I should never breathe the outer air or see a human face again."

"But that chain is a mere nothing," said Mrs. Bunting. "Let me cut it."

"You cannot—no one can cut it," replied Frenhina. "Nothing can unrivet it except the enchanted quartz hammer with which it was fastened on; and that the King of the Mines keeps in his own cavern, and he must be a bold man who should try to take it from thence."

"But the King would try, I am sure," said Owen's mother. "Let us send him a message. My husband would go."

"Please do not," exclaimed Frenhina. "Do you think that I have not considered all this, and turned over every plan? The very eagerness of the King to release me would be his undoing, for if he lost command of himself for a moment, the metal-king would have the mastery of him as he had over me, and would enslave him too. Neither would it do for a person to attempt it who does not care about me, for every kind of terror and temptation will be put in his way. So, you see, there is no hope for me," concluded Frenhina. "And if I could but know that the King is happy and contented without me, I should be resigned to live and die the humpbacked slave that I am."

Frenhina put up her hand to hide a tear that would fall as she spoke: and the two women sat silent until Owen's voice asking for a little water roused them from their thoughts.

A few days after this conversation Owen was led triumphantly into the sitting-room. His next grand achievement was a walk in the garden, with his father on one side of him and his brother on the other ; and before another week was over he was able to go to school again as usual.

Owen had always been a thoughtful boy and fond of his book, but now he would sit pondering over his books so intently and so long, that more than once the Captain shook his head and said to himself, " That boy has not got over his fever yet."

It was neither illness nor his books, however, that made Owen so quiet. He had heard his mother's conversation with Frenhina, hardly knowing at the time whether it was a dream or not ; and ever since he had been thinking, thinking, how to set Frenhina, his kind lady, free.

One evening just after sunset, when Frenhina was gone back to her work in the mountain caverns, and Owen and his mother were sitting alone, he said, " Mother, don't you think I am quite strong again ?"

" Yes, my boy, and very much grown too. But why do you ask ?" said his mother.

" Because," said Owen, and there he paused. " Mother, it is because I heard your talk with the Lady Frenhina that day —you know ?"

" I know," said his mother. "And you want to set her free."

" That's it !" cried Owen, much relieved. " May I try ? You see I shall be in earnest to do it, and yet I think I could keep my temper, and not let the King of the Mines have power over me."

" I think you could, my son ; and I have been considering whether or not to propose the adventure to you."

Owen jumped up joyfully. "Oh thank you, mother! Then I will go to-night. Father will be out all night with the keepers watching for that gang of poachers, and John and Nelly need not know where I am gone."

"But you have neither sword nor shield ready," said his mother.

"I don't suppose arms would be of any use against magic," replied Owen. "I shall be as careful and steady as I can, and the sooner I go the better; so good-bye, mother."

Owen went into the coal-hole, from whence Frenhina always seemed to come, and found a little passage at the back so narrow that he had to drag himself along in the darkness on his face. Gradually it grew larger, so that he could crawl, and then shuffle, and at last walk along upright. By-and-by he saw a glimmering light in the distance, and as he approached it along his uneven path he found that it proceeded from an enormous furnace, round which strange misshapen imps, which looked as if they were made of molten lead and jagged lumps of ore instead of flesh and bone, were busily working. Some were pouring liquid gold into rock-cauldrons with enormous ladles, others blowing the furnace, others beating out or pouring off the glowing metals, and none of them seemed to heed the heat which Owen could hardly bear even at the entrance of the cave. He looked in vain for Frenhina among these grimy imps. As one of them passed near him with a mass of glowing iron in his tongs, Owen called out to him, "I say, where is the King of the Mines?"

The dwarf looked up at him with a grin. "Ha, ha! look

here, comrades; here's another slave of the above-ground creatures come in to join us."

" Ho, ho," replied the rest.   " He looks strong, we will set him to blow the bellows.   Won't he like it—ha !"

" Where's your master ?" said Owen, not much liking the way they were crowding about him.

" You'll see him soon enough," replied the first dwarf, grinning again.   " Better go back the way you came—if you can find it !"

Owen looked round, and saw that he was indeed in a perfect network of dark vaulted passages.   Black water oozed from the roof and trickled down the rocky sides, and here and there a vein of precious ore sparkled in the firelight.   He thought he saw a gleam, as from the mouth of another cavern, down one of these dismal tunnels, and was just going towards it, when his eye fell on an unfortunate bat which lay a prisoner near him, with its wing caught under a great stone.   Owen could never pass by a creature in distress, and anxious as he was to get on, he laboured at the stone with hand and knee, amid shouts of mockery from the impish smiths, until he had succeeded in raising it, and the bat flew joyfully up and wheeled round his head as he walked on.   The light that he had noticed did come from a cave, and in it he saw Frenhina herself, with heaps of pure silver about her, her delicate fingers at work on some fairy-like frost-work.   She did not perceive Owen, for her back was towards him, and he was hesitating whether to speak to her or not, when a gleaming light in the distance made him look round.   It was a dwarfish figure like the rest, but from the golden crown on its head Owen judged that it must be the King of the Mines himself, and he hastened towards him along the slippery vault.

The figure retreated, but Owen pursued, and tracked him into a strange weird-looking cavern, so vast and dark that Owen could see neither the roof nor the end, only the gleam of the great pillars of precious metal that supported it vanishing in the far-off gloom. The only light in that strange abode seemed to come from the King of the Mines himself. His face glowed as though it were made of a mass of red-hot copper, from which his eyes gleamed like two small flames. His dress seemed to be made of half-melted gold, and his hands had the same hideous red-hot glow as his face. His hair and beard were like red-hot copper wire. In his belt Owen saw the enchanted quartz hammer that could set Frenhina free.

Owen had never seen such a strange figure before, and he stood gazing at him until the King of the Mines, turning his flaming eyes upon him, said in a hollow voice:

"What are you doing here, little boy?"

"If you are the King of the Mines, I came to look for you," replied Owen.

"You!" said the metal-king, contemptuously. "What can such as you want with me?"

"Well, I want your quartz hammer," said Owen.

Then the king flew into a rage, and called him all manner of names, and threatened him with the severest punishments if he did not go away at once, and never venture there again.

Owen stood quiet, knowing that as long as he kept his temper the king had no power over him. As soon as he had a chance to be heard he told him that he should not go unless the Lady Frenhina went with him.

The king raged more than ever. Then, suddenly changing his tone, he said: "You are a fine little fellow. Not many would have stood so fearlessly; I only spoke like this to try you. Come, I want such a lad as you. Stay with me and you shall be my heir. I will clothe you in cloth of gold, and all my servants shall be at your beck and call, and all the wealth of the world shall be yours. Only look what I will give you." And the king, leading him aside, showed him such heaped-up treasures of gold and precious stones, that it seemed as if the whole mountain must be made of them. But Owen's thoughts were full of the captive Frenhina, and none of the metal-king's offers could tempt him.

"It is of no use your trying to turn me from my purpose," he said. "I want nothing but the Lady Frenhina, and I will not leave off trying until I have freed her."

Then the King of the Mines went into such a furious passion that his face and beard glowed until Owen felt his hair lifted by the heat from them. Not a step would he draw back, however, although the metal-king glowed hotter and hotter, until his whole body was a transparent ball of fire, with blue flames flickering up round it, and the quartz hammer in the midst. With a sudden impulse, Owen plunged his hand into the molten mass, and grasping the quartz hammer, drew it out unscathed. And with a report like a hundred cannon the

King of the Mines blew up, and the explosion rolled in thunder from chamber to chamber of his cavern home, shaking the solid mountain to the roots, and bringing down huge masses of rock all round the astonished boy. He stood uncrushed, for the quartz hammer was in his hand ; but there arose around him so great a dust and sulphurous smell that he was all but suffocated. Then there was a rush of wings, and a flight of bats led by the one he had set free came wheeling round his head and fanned him with outspread wings, until the dust had settled and all was quiet again.

Then Owen perceived that the nail which riveted the hammer was a blazing diamond, whose light showed him that masses of rock were piled all round him, and his path quite lost. He tried to climb over them, but could not. Then it struck him that he would try the hammer's power ; and at the first tap the rocks fell apart, and Owen passed on without difficulty between them. He made straight for Frenhina's cave, and running in too eager even to speak, he stooped down, and with one stroke of the hammer the chain shrivelled away like a scorching hair, and Frenhina was free. But was it Frenhina? For when he looked up, a beautiful lady in shining robes, tall and stately as a white lily, stooped to embrace him, calling him her kind brave boy. Yes, it was his own lady's face, and her own sweet voice.

"But how beautiful you are!" cried Owen. "Oh, how glad mother will be! Make haste, and let us come to her."

And they passed hand-in-hand from the heart of the hill, led by the diamond light.

G

There was joy in the little house under the hill that night; but in the royal palace not far off there was sorrow and dismay. Servants and noblemen jostled one another in the halls, and grave doctors whispered together and shook their heads. For the King had long been languishing, and now he was dying, all for love of a lady who was either dead or false to him. In the midst of this confusion a tall veiled figure entered the palace gates, led by a boy in a common schoolboy dress, and with a small hammer in his hand.

"You cannot come here to-night," said one of the servants, as he passed; "the King, our master, is dying."

"Never mind," said the boy, drawing his companion on; "but come to him. You saved my life, and I am sure you can save his."

So they passed through the groups of attendants, too anxious to pay any attention to them, and made their way to the royal bedchamber.

"He is dying," said one of the doctors by the bedside; "he no longer takes notice of anything."

The veiled lady pushed him gently aside, and throwing back the mantle that hid her shining robes she said, "Look up, my King, my betrothed, for your Frenhina is come to you at last."

And the light returned to the King's eyes and the colour to his cheeks, for Frenhina's presence was the only medicine that he had needed. And instead of sorrow and dismay, the palace was full of joyful preparations for the wedding festival.

You may be sure that the Buntings were not forgotten.

Captain Bunting was made Lord Chief Ranger of the Woods and Forests, which was a post that exactly suited him. Mrs. Bunting was Housekeeper in ordinary to her Majesty, and Superintendent of the Royal Dairy. Nelly was appointed one of the maids of honour, but before long she married a young nobleman and went to live with him on his estate. On her marriage she made a holiday and merry-making for all the silk-weavers in the kingdom. John, who had shown a strong turn for business, became a great merchant, and his ships traded to all lands.

The little house under the hill was not quite forsaken. For when the royal wedding took place, the Postmaster-General determined to put a new purple silk lining to the King's post-bag in honour of the occasion; and when the old one was ripped out, there lay Captain Bunting's missing letter, limp and yellow with its ten years' solitary confinement. And the King and his council voted the hill that had been inhabited by the King of the Mines to Captain Bunting for his gallant services; and he sank a mine there, and dug from it treasure enough to make his family a prosperous one for many generations.

But Owen, the author of all this good fortune, what was to be done for him? " Come and live with us and be our son, and reign after us," said Frenhina to him; "for it is to you that we owe our lives and all our happiness. Besides, have you not belonged to me ever since you were Baby Bunting, and I used to come and sing to you while your mother was out milking ?"

" I should like to live with you," said Owen, but I will not be your heir, for that would not be fair or just. What I should really like is that you should give me a good education to fit me for it, and then make me one of your ministers, to help to rule the land, and to make the people as good and as happy as possible.

" Owen," said the King, " you have chosen nobly, and your wish shall be fulfilled."

So Baby Bunting grew up to be a wise and a learned statesman. And I cannot tell which was the happiest—the nation whom he governed, or the King and Queen whom he served, or Owen himself, the respected and beloved Prime Minister.

DAPPLE-GREY.

Page 197.

XII.—DAPPLE-GREY.

" I had a little pony, they called him Dapple-grey,
I lent him to a lady to ride a mile away.
She whipped him, she slashed him, she rode him through the mire :
I would not lend my horse again for all the lady's hire."

THERE was once a boy named Philip, who lived in a little cottage in the middle of a wood. He had lived there for many years with his father, but the old man died at last ; and on his deathbed he told his son that if he had not been cruelly wronged he might have left him a large house and wide lands, but that now he had nothing to leave him except the cottage and his little pony. And he begged him to be kind to the pony for his sake. After his father's death, Philip had no companion but the pony, and very fond of one another they were. The pony was white, spotted and dappled all over with grey, and therefore he was called Dapple-grey. Now Dapple-grey was very useful to his young master, for Philip used to pick up dry sticks in the wood and tie them into faggots, and carry them into the nearest town on Dapple-grey's back, where the people bought them to light their fires with. Or sometimes he and Dapple-grey would take a long trip to the moor, and bring back heather for making brooms, or dry fern for making beds for the cattle. With the money that they earned in this way, Philip would buy bread and clothes for himself, and corn for Dapple-grey. So they lived very happily together, although they had to work very hard in order to earn enough to live on.

One day when Philip had sold all his pony-load of faggots, and he and Dapple-grey were just going to leave the town and go home to their cottage, a grandly-dressed lady came up to him and said, "Is this your pony?"

"Yes, he is mine," said Philip, patting Dapple-grey's sleek shoulder.

"He does not look a bad pony," said the lady. "I will give you a shilling if you will lend him to me for half-an-hour. I have to go a mile away to see one of my fields, and I am afraid of dirtying my boots"—for she had very smart red boots on, with gilt laces.

Philip had never parted with his pony before, and he hesitated for some time. But a shilling was more than he could earn in a whole week, and he certainly did very much want some money to buy a new jacket before the cold weather came. So he said to the lady: "Will you be very kind to my pony if I let you have him? And will you ride him gently, and not whip him? for he never has been whipped in his life."

"Oh, of course!" said the lady; and up she got and away she rode.

"Who is that lady?" said Philip to the woman who had bought his last faggot.

"Don't you know?" replied the woman. "She is Mrs.

Hippoharpy. She lives in the grand house up there, and she is the richest and most powerful person in the country."

"I hope she will be kind to Dapple-grey," said Philip.

He waited very anxiously until he saw the lady coming back on Dapple-grey. She jumped off and flung him the shilling, and went away in such a hurry that he had not even time to thank her. But I do not think he would have done so if he could ; for when he came to look at Dapple-grey, he was panting and hot and tired, and splashed with mud from head to foot, and there were marks of cuts and slashes from a whip all over his pretty dappled sides and legs. Philip patted and comforted poor Dapple-grey as well as he could, and he walked home with his arm over his pony's neck, singing :

> " I had a little pony, they called him Dapple-grey,
>   I lent him to a lady to ride a mile away.
>   She whipped him, she slashed him, she rode him through the mire :
>   I would not lend my horse again for all the lady's hire."

The next time that Philip came to the town to sell faggots the lady met him again.

"Oh, here you are !" said she. "Now give me your pony quickly, for I want him again."

"I cannot let you have my pony," said Philip.

"Why not ?" said Mrs. Hippoharpy. "I will give you a shilling."

"I will not lend him you for all your hire," said Philip, " because you whipped him."

"Oh nonsense !" said the lady. "Do not be so foolish. I will give you two shillings."

"I will not lend him for all the money you have got," said Philip ; and he walked away. And Dapple-grey rubbed his nose against Philip's arm as they went.

When the lady saw that Philip would not lend her the pony, she stamped in her fine red boots, and called out after him, "You will repent it !"

And before Philip could reach the wood, five servants in Mrs. Hippoharpy's livery rushed upon him, tied his hands behind him, and led him and Dapple-grey prisoners to the great house. Dapple-grey was put into Mrs. Hippoharpy's stable, and Philip was set to break stones to mend the road through the park.

Poor Philip was nearly heartbroken when he saw Mrs. Hippoharpy riding by the next morning on Dapple-grey, and the pony neighed and struggled to come to him until the lady whipped him so that he was obliged to go on. But there was no one to help them, for Mrs. Hippoharpy was so rich that nobody dared to say a word against anything that she did. So Philip went on breaking stones.

One day when Philip was going knock, knock, knock with his heavy hammer upon the stones, he began to keep time to it by singing :

"I had a little pony, they called him Dapple-grey,
I lent him to a lady to ride a mile away.
She whipped him, she slashed him, she rode him through the mire :
I would not lend my horse again for all the lady's hire.

"But when I told the lady, 'I won't lend Dapple-grey,'
O then she was so angry, she took him quite away.
She whipped him, she slashed him, she rode him through the mire,
She set me to break stones here, and gave me nought for hire."

"Mr. Philip, I am very sorry for you," said a small piping voice, as soon as he had finished.

"Why, what was that?" said Philip. And he looked up and down, and to and fro; but no one could he see, far or near. "Perhaps it was only my fancy," thought Philip; and he began to sing again—

"I had a little pony,"

But scarcely had he done his song when,

"Mr. Philip, indeed I am very sorry for you," said the small piping voice again.

Philip looked up and down and to and fro; until on a bramble branch just over his heap of stones he saw a little robin sitting watching him, with its head on one side.

"Halloo! was that you?" said Philip.

"Yes, that is me," said the robin, bowing and bobbing and jerking his tail until he nearly jerked himself off the bramble branch.

"What can I do to help you?" added he, in his small piping voice.

"I am much obliged to you," said Philip, "but I don't think you can do anything for me."

"Can't I, though?" said the robin, jerking his tail very hard. "Come, what do you want done?"

"Why, I want to get my dear Dapple-grey back again."

"Very well," said the robin; "and if I get him back for you, will you do whatever I ask you?"

"Yes, that I will," said Philip.

"Very well," piped the robin again. "Then when the dinner-bell rings to-day, do not you go in to dinner with the other servants, but hide yourself under the bushes outside the stable-yard, and you shall see what will happen."

Philip promised, and the robin immediately flew away to the stable where Dapple-grey was kept. The door happened to be open, for the groom was sweeping out the stable. The robin busily fetched a quantity of little sticks and straws, which he laid on the top of the door near the hinge, and then went and waited inside the stable. But the groom never observed him ; so when he had done his job he went out and pulled the door after him, and turned the key and put it into his pocket. This his mistress had told him always to do, for fear Dapple-grey should be stolen away. But he did not see that the robin's bits of stick prevented the door from shutting close, so that when he turned the key the lock stuck harmlessly out, without fastening anything at all.

When the robin saw that this part of his plan had succeeded, he jerked his tail for pleasure, and flying to Dapple-grey, began to peck and claw at the knot which fastened his halter. Dapple-grey watched him as if he understood it all. But the knot would not come undone, and the robin ws nearly tired out, when a little squeaky voice close to him said, "Shall I help you, Robin ?"

The robin looked round, and saw a little brown mouse running along the edge of the manger.

"O yes, good Mousey ; bite this knot in two for me," he said.

"And if I do you this service, will you do me a service in return ?" said the mouse.

"To be sure I will," replied the robin, "only be quick."

Then the mouse ran along the halter, and very soon gnawed it through. As soon as Dapple-grey saw that he was loose, he ran to the door and pawed it open with his hoof, and trotted out with the robin flying after.

"Stop, stop !" cried the mouse, who could not go so fast. "You promised to do me a service now."

But the robin was so busy trying to keep up with Dapple-grey that he did not hear the mouse's little squeaky voice, and so on they went. And Philip sprang out from the bushes and jumped joyfully upon his pony's back, and Dapple-grey neighed as they galloped away.

"Stop, stop !" cried the robin, "we have not half finished. You promised to do whatever I asked."

But Philip was so busy running away from Mrs. Hippoharpy that he did not hear the robin's small piping voice. So on they went, and never stopped until they reached the cottage in the middle of the wood. Then Philip jumped down, and he and his pony rubbed noses together for nearly ten minutes without stopping.

"There now," piped the robin, flying up quite out of breath, "why did you not stop when I called you ? Now we shall have to go all the way back again."

"What for ?" said Philip.

"Why, would you not like to punish Mrs. Hippoharpy, and to prevent her ever getting Dapple-grey back again ?"

"Yes, very much," said Philip.

"Then please to pull out the longest feather in my tail," said the robin.

"What an odd thing to ask!" said Philip.   "No, indeed I will not.   I should hurt you if I did."

"But please do," persisted the robin.   You promised to do whatever I asked."

Then Philip took hold of the longest feather in the robin's tail, and pulled it out.   And behold, instead of a feather, he held in his hand a small, beautiful bright steel sword, with a golden hilt.   And instead of a robin, there stood before him a tall serving man in a red velvet waistcoat, who bowed to him and said : "Thank you, Mr. Philip.   Now I am Robin the man, and no longer Robin the bird; and I will serve you as faithfully as I served your father before you."

As they walked back to the great house, Philip still riding on Dapple-grey, Robin—for that really was his name—told Philip that his father had once been lord of the country and owner of that great house, until Mrs. Hippoharpy came and wickedly turned him out by means of an enchanted willow-wand which she had.   "I was your father's own serving man," continued Robin.   "The other servants all ran away except the groom and myself.   We fought to the last; and she turned me into a bird with her wand, but what became of the groom I cannot tell."

"But when I go and claim my rights, perhaps she will turn me into a frog or a spider," said Philip.

"You need not fear," replied Robin; "for round the wand there is written—

> ' Wand of willow shall not quail
> Save at sword from robin's tail.'

This is why she never dares to bring the wand out of doors with her, or she would have turned you into something before now. When you meet her, wave the sword that you drew from my tail over her head, and her wand will have no power to hurt you."

So they came boldly up to the door, and Philip said to the porter, " I want to see your mistress."

"She does not see beggar boys," said the porter.

"But she must see me," said Philip.

"What are you doing here ? Go back and break stones," said the porter, "or I will have you flogged."

Then Robin stepped forward in his red velvet waistcoat and held the porter fast by his collar, while Philip marched straight into the hall where Mrs. Hippoharpy was sitting at dinner. As soon as she saw him, she cried, "Get along with you, or I will turn you into a horse-fly !" And she brandished the willow-wand.

But Philip waved his sword and answered,

> " Wand of willow, fear and fail,
> Here is sword from robin's tail !"

And the willow-wand blackened and shrivelled, and fell in little pieces at her feet. Then Mrs. Hippoharpy screamed and ran to the window and jumped out, and fled away through the park and across the fields, and away, away, far out of sight.

The same moment that the wand shrivelled, Robin found that he was no longer holding the porter by the throat, but a big bumble-bee. And all the other servants turned back into flies and wasps and ants; for Mrs. Hippoharpy had turned them into servants for herself by the power of her wand. So there was no one to dispute Philip's right to his father's house. He was just going in to take possession, when he felt something running on his foot, and on looking down he saw that it was a little brown mouse.

"Oh, I had forgotten him," said Robin. "That is the mouse that gnawed Dapple-grey's halter in two, and I promised to do him a service."

"What do you want done for you, Mousey?" said Philip.

"Please to cut off my tail with your sword," replied the mouse's little squeaky voice.

"Certainly, if you wish it," said Philip. "I wonder what you will turn into."

And behold, as soon as his tail was cut off, the mouse turned into a tidy little groom in a brown fustian suit, and his tail turned into a stable broom.

"That is capital!" cried Philip. "Now you shall take care of Dapple-grey."

All the other old servants who had run away, when they heard that their own master's son was come back, came and begged to be taken into his service.

So Philip became the richest and most powerful person in

all the country. Never had there been a better master than he, or better servants than Robin and Mousey ; and never was pony better groomed and fed and tended than Dapple-grey was from that time forth.

And the robin's-tail-sword hangs in a glass case over the hall chimney-piece to this day.

XIII.—RIDE A COCK-HORSE.

" Ride a cock-horse
To Banbury Cross,
To see an old woman ride on a black horse;
With rings on her fingers,
And bells on her toes,
And she shall have music wherever she goes."

AND this old woman was no other than Mrs. Hippoharpy herself. When she had jumped out of the window and fled away over the fields, she ran and ran until she came to the town of Banbury. And there she stopped, because she could run no longer. She had a few pounds in her pocket, and with them she hired a room to live in. But she had never been accustomed to keep under her temper or to master her passions, and so the sudden shock of losing her enchanted wand had such an effect on her that she became quite daft and silly, and the people of Banbury always called her Crazy Mistress Hippoharpy.

Before long all her money was spent, and she must have died of hunger if Philip had not chanced to hear of her. Now he had learnt to master his passions, so instead of wishing to punish Mrs. Hippoharpy for the harm she had done him, he pitied her miserable state, and sent to ask what he could do

BANBURY CROSS.

for her. They told him that she had no money, and that what she wanted most was a horse, for the poor silly old woman would sit and cry in her chair half the day because she had no horse now to ride.

" Then she shall have one," said Philip, " and enough money to live on too. Mousey, take the strong black horse that Mrs. Hippoharpy used to ride before she took Dapple-grey, and ride him over to Banbury. Find him a good stable there, and tell the man who has the care of him that Mrs. Hippoharpy may ride him every day ; but she must not ride him far or fast, and she is never to be allowed a whip."

For he remembered how she had whipped Dapple-grey.

So Mousey, the groom, rode the black horse to Banbury. He did not much like his errand, for he thought that Mrs. Hippoharpy did not deserve to have him. But when the old woman saw the horse, she jumped up and down on the pavement for a quarter of an hour for very joy, and then she took a ride.

Now the more people there were to look at her, the better Mrs. Hippoharpy was pleased. So she never cared to go beyond the town, but always rode round and round and round the square in the middle of which Banbury Cross stands.

You know that she had quite lost her mind ; and one of her crazy fancies was that she was still rich and powerful, and that all the nobles in the land were wanting to marry her. So she put a quantity of rings on her fingers, which she said were her wedding-rings, for that she was married to them all. And in order that they might hear her passing by, and might come

P

out to join her, she sewed rows of little jingling bells to the toes of her red boots that had once been so smart. It was lucky that she liked being stared at; for all the little boys in Banbury soon knew the story of Philip and Dapple-grey. And they got hobby-horses, painted as like Dapple-grey as possible, and whenever the crazy old woman went out to ride, they would come riding on their hobby-horses up all the streets and alleys to Banbury Cross to see her. And as they rode along they would call to one another to follow, saying :—

> " Ride a cock-horse
> To Banbury Cross,
> To see an old woman ride on a black horse;
> With rings on her fingers,
> And bells on her toes,
> And she shall have music wherever she goes !"

XIV.—HUSH-A-BYE BABY.

ONCE upon a time there was a countess whose husband was killed in the wars, and her own house burnt over her head by the enemy, so that she had to run away by night with her baby in her arms. She fled away, not knowing where she went, until she came to a deserted hut hidden in some trees by the side of a stream; and here she determined to stay until the enemy should leave the country. She had saved nothing from her burning house except her baby, and a little silver cross which she hung round the baby's neck. So she tried to get her living by weaving baskets of rushes and filling them with the wild strawberries that grew on the river bank. These she sold in a town that was near her hiding-place.

She had made a cradle of rushes for her baby, and while she wove her baskets, or gathered her strawberries, she hung the baby in its cradle to the branch of a young ash-tree that grew near the stream.   And the wind rocked it to and fro, and rocked the baby to sleep, while the mother sang to it—

> " Hush-a-bye baby
> On the tree-top.
> When the wind blows,
> The cradle will rock.
> When the bough breaks,
> The cradle will fall ;
> Down will come cradle and baby and all !"

But she never thought that this would really happen, for the branch was tough and strong, and waved gently over the child as though it liked its burden.

One day the countess had wandered farther than usual in search of wild strawberries, when she heard in the distance a sound of drums beating and people shouting.   She called out to a woodman who was running past : " What is this noise of drums and shouting that I hear ?"

" It is the Earl of Castello Marino's army," replied the woodman.   " He has driven away the enemy who killed his sister, and is now marching home again."

" Oh, it is my brother !" cried the countess.   " Which way is he gone ?"

" Out yonder," said the woodman ; " but make haste if you want to see him, for the army is already gone by."   And then he ran on.

The countess looked back.   She was already some way from where her baby was sleeping.   If she ran back to fetch it, she should never be able to catch her brother before he passed out of reach ; and she must make the long journey to his castle on foot, and perhaps her baby might die of cold and hunger on the way. The shouts were already dying away in the distance. She looked back once more, and cried—

> " O waving trees, O rushing water,
> Guard from harm my little daughter !"

And then she ran as fast as she could after the army. But when she reached it, they told her that the earl was being carried on in front in a litter, badly wounded. So she ran on again, but it was hard work, and it took her a longer time than she had thought to get to him. The wounded earl was very glad to see his sister, whom he had believed to be dead ; and he made his army halt, and sent back ten of his body-guard with the countess to fetch her little daughter. But as they were going back the wind rose and a storm came on, and the mother was sadly alarmed for her baby. And when they got to the place where she had left it, behold the bough was broken with the wind, and cradle and baby and all were gone. Not a trace of it was left, only one of the soldiers after searching down the stream brought back a bit of the broken cradle which he had found caught in the hanging branch of a willow. The poor mother sat down and wept, and wrung her hands and said—

> " O faithless trees, O cruel water,
> To guard so ill my little daughter !"

And the trees sighed and tossed their arms, and the waters sobbed and murmured. But if the countess could have understood what they said, they would have told her that they had done all they could for the baby. For when the strong wind came and broke the bough, the ash-tree tossed the cradle out towards the stream, which raised its white arms and caught the child, and carried it safely over rock and stone as it rushed foaming on.

But the baby must soon have been drowned, for the stream could hold it up no longer, if it had not chanced that a Water-nymph wandered that morning up from the sea to gather some water-lilies that bloomed in a still, shady bend of the stream. She saw the little baby just as it was sinking, and caught it gently in her arms and bore it down to the sea, and into a cave which no one knew of but herself. She knew that the little human baby could not live under water as sea-nymphs can, so she made it a bed of cotton-rush, and brought it the daintiest food she could prepare, and nursed and tended it in the secret cave. And the little girl throve and grew until she could run about with her little bare feet on the white sandy shore of the cave, and play with the crimson sea-weed and many coloured shells which her kind foster-mother brought her.

The sea nymph called her little charge Rivula, because she had found her in the river. Little Rivula could not remember her own mother, or the time when she rocked on the tree top, and she lived very happily in the cave with the kind friend who had saved her. Often on a fine moonlight night, the sea-nymph would take Rivula in her arms and float with her far out to sea, while she sang to her of shining gems and coral caves, far beneath the dark blue waves. And the phosphorus-light parted round them and closed again, and the cliffs looked dim and dreamlike, and Rivula thought that there never was anything more beautiful or more enchanting.

When the tide was low, Rivula would come out and wander among the rocks or along the wooded banks of the stream, but she always went back to her cave again before the tide came in.

As years went on, a report was spread abroad that the coast was haunted, for now and then sailor boys wandering along the shore had caught sight of Rivula's white dress in the distance ; or fishermen sailing home at night had heard snatches of the sea-nymph's song. So the country people did not like to go near the place, and Rivula wandered undisturbed.

Not far from Rivula's secret cave there stood a castle in which a young earl lived. When he was quite a boy his father had died of a wound that he received in war, and his mother died of grief soon after. He was brought up by a widowed countess who was his aunt ; but though she was very kind, she was always sad. People said that she had never got over the death of her only child, whom she had lost in some sad way. And the young earl having no other companion felt lonely in his grand castle and splendid gardens, and he took to wandering for hours about the country. In one of his rambles he met an old fisherman, who warned him not to go any further along the coast, because it was haunted by an old witch who was so much feared that nobody dared go near her.

The young earl immediately made up his mind to go and find the witch, and went straight to the haunted coast. He looked for her all that day and for many other days in vain. Once he thought he saw something flutter behind a rock, but when he reached the place it was gone. At last one spring-tide he clambered round into a little bay that he had never been able to reach before, and there he beheld, not the wrinkled old witch that he expected to find, but a beautiful bare-footed maiden. She was bending over a clear rocky pool which she had made into a little ocean-garden by planting it with bright-coloured seaweeds and fernlike coralline. So busy was she with it that she did not see the young earl until he came quite close to her. Rivula had never seen a man before; but he looked so kind and spoke so gently that she was not at all afraid, and before they parted she had shown him all her treasures; the sandpiper's nest with its five round eggs; the little silver-scaled fish that she had found nearly dead on the shore, and had nursed in her garden pool until he was well and merry again; and the queer old hermit crab who lived in a little cave of his own, and never came out except to mow the green grass-like seaweed with his strong hooked claw.

Rivula never was lonely, for she made friends with all the birds and fishes round her, and gave them names and fed them, until they were so tame they would come at her call.

The young earl was delighted with her, and promised to come again the next day and bring her rare fruits and flowers from his hot-houses.

"Dear mother," said Rivula to the sea-nymph that evening,

"you told me to beware of men because they were often rude
and rough ; but one came to me to-day, and he is so kind and
beautiful I should like him to be always with me."

And the sea-nymph, who had watched them from a creek
close by, smiled as she combed Rivula's shining hair, and sang
her a song that she had never heard before, of a merman who
had found her lost amid the drifting foam, and had thrown his
arms around her, loved, and made for her a home. Some days
after this Rivula told the sea-nymph that the young earl had
asked her to go and live with him in his castle.

"Did you say you would go ?" asked the sea-nymph.

"And leave my dear ocean-mother ?" said Rivula. "O no.
I told him that I could never leave you. And yet I did not
like saying No, because it made him sorry."

"You need not say No, my child," said the kind sea-nymph.
"You know that all my kindred live far away in warm seas
where feathery palm-trees wave above their coral reefs. They
have long wanted me home, and only yesterday a porpoise
brought me a pressing message from them to come. So you
shall marry the earl, and I will go back to my kindred, and
every summer I will come and visit my child in her grand
castle by the sea."

The young earl was rejoiced when Rivula told him the
next morning that she would come to him, and he hastened to
make ready the castle for his bride.

When the wedding morning came, he went down to the
shore to meet her ; but he would hardly have known his bare-
footed damsel in the beautiful maiden who came towards him.

She wore a wonderful lace veil, woven by the sea-fairies of the finest and whitest corallines ; her shoes were of the most delicate mother-of-pearl, her robe was trimmed with petrified foam-flakes, and on her shining hair was placed a coronet of pearls. She wore no ornaments but pearls, except that beneath the splendid pearl necklace there hung the little silver cross that her mother had tied round her neck when she was a baby, cradled on the tree-top.

All the earl's vassals shouted for joy when he led in his lovely bride. The widowed countess was waiting on the steps to welcome her. But when she saw the little silver cross, she threw her arms round Rivula's neck, crying, " O my child, my little daughter whom I lost !"

She was indeed Rivula's mother. After searching in vain for the baby that the wind had tossed from the broken tree-top, the soldiers who were with the countess had brought her to the castle of her brother the wounded earl. When he died, she had stayed to take care of his little boy, now the young earl who had married her daughter. So Rivula was comforted for the loss of her kind sea-nymph friend by the love of her own dear mother.

And every year, when summer seas grew warm, there came a sound of sweet and wondrous singing across the starlit waves, and Rivula flew down the terrace steps to greet her ocean-mother once again.

In course of time the earl and his fair wife were blessed with several children. The widowed countess loved them so dearly that they were hardly ever away from her. Every evening she lulled them to sleep with the song that she had sung to their mother years ago.

> " Hush-a-bye baby
> On the tree-top.
> When the wind blows,
> The cradle will rock.
> When the bough breaks,
> The cradle will fall ;
> Down will come cradle and baby and all !"

And thus it is that the countess's song became a nursery lullaby.

XV.—AN OLD WOMAN WHO LIVED IN A SHOE.

" There was an old woman who lived in a shoe,
   She had so many children she didn't know what to do.
   She gave them some broth without any bread,
   She whipped them all soundly and sent them to bed.

I T was no common shoe, that you may be sure of, in which an old woman and seventeen children could live. And they had not always lived there. Once they had had a house that stood in the valley at the edge of the forest, and above a beautiful lake round which the mountains rose so high that their heads were always capped with snow. Here the seventeen children lived happily with their father and with the old woman who was their nurse.

But across the mountains in the next valley to the one they lived in, was the castle of a great big giant named Groszfusz. And very early one morning this giant passed by, as he was going home after supping with another giant. Now Giant Groszfusz was in a very bad temper, for the morning air was chilly, and his supper had disagreed with him, and he had quarrelled with the other giant and had had a box on the ear. So when he saw this comfortable little house, he gave it such a kick with his great foot that he kicked the roof right off, and

AN OLD WOMAN WHO LIVED IN A SHOE.

Page 220.

there lay the father and all his children in bed. You may fancy that they did not stay there, however, when they saw the roof right off, and the giant's great ugly face grinning in at them.

The children ran away very fast out of the house, while their father snatched up his sword to defend them. " Ho!" roared the giant, " You will fight, will you ?"

And he took him up and put him into his waistcoat pocket. Then he looked about for the children, but they crept away under the gooseberry trees in the garden, so that he scratched his great fingers in trying to catch them. And their father scrambled out of the giant's pocket on to his shoulder, and began cutting away at the giant's face with his sword.

"Oh, oh! the bees are stinging me," roared the giant. And with one dash of his club he made the house a heap of ruins, and then ran away over the mountains, still puffing and fighting at the bees that he thought were attacking him. But he carried the children's father away with him ; and there stood the seventeen children with their father gone, and their house in ruins, and the old nurse sitting crying over the broken bits of the best china tea-cups.

Now when the giant gave that great kick to the roof of the house, he kicked the latchet of his shoe in two. And as he ran away the shoe came off his foot, but on he went, leaving it behind him in the valley.

Since they had no other place to go to, the nurse and children took possession of the shoe. The bigger boys thatched over the top, and cut a little door in the side-leather, and there they all lived in the shoe. The two eldest, Tapfer and Huldrich, were boys, then came a girl named Guta, then a third boy named Witikind, then three more girls, and the rest were all little ones. Tapfer was a fine, brave fellow, very tall and strong. He used to cut wood in the forest for the fires, and to fetch water from the stream, and to do all the hardest work of the household. Huldrich was strong and brave too, but of a gentler nature than his brother. He dug the potatoes and cut the cabbages, and attended to the garden and the two goats. Witikind was a little fellow for his age, but very sharp and full of plans and contrivances. His business was to catch fish and game to supply them with meat for dinner. As for Guta, the eldest girl, she looked after the little ones and helped every one, and was always busy.

Now the reason why the old nurse gave them their broth once without any bread, and whipped them all soundly and sent them to bed, was as follows.

Witikind was out fishing in the lake with a net, and he caught a large fish, but in dragging the net to land it got entangled in the stump of an old tree that stood half under the water, and pull as hard as Witikind might, he was not strong enough to pull it free again. He ran home to the shoe to get some one to help him ; but Tapfer was gone up the mountain side to cut grass for the goats, Huldrich was driving them home to be milked, Nurse was washing clothes at the stream, and the children were all out gathering dewberries under Guta's care. So there was nobody at home. But on the table lay the bread-knife, and Witikind thought it would help him capitally, and he caught it up and ran off for fear his big fish should escape. He began cutting away with the knife at the branch that entangled his net, but just as he had almost cut it through, snap went the knife, and down went the broken bits into the water. Now it was the only knife they had, for almost all their things had been destroyed when the house tumbled down. So Witikind picked up the broken bits and his nets and the big fish, and walked back to the shoe sadly enough. He found them all come home, and everybody hunting for the knife that they might begin their supper. The children had come in tired and hungry, and the old nurse had been scolding Guta for keeping them out so long. When she saw the broken knife she said, "O you naughty, naughty boy! what will you spoil next? I never did see such tiresome children as you, and there are so many of you I don't know what to do. You don't expect to have any bread for supper, do you, when there isn't a knife left to cut it? No, there is the broth that I have got ready for you, but not a bit of bread shall you have. And here has Huldrich burst a hole in his shoe with digging, and the children have torn their clothes in the forest, and Tapfer has not brought me in a bit of wood to day. I really don't know which is the worst among you, so I shall just whip you all soundly and send you to bed." And so she did.

The bedroom of the three eldest boys was in the very toe of the boot, and a very dark corner it would have been if a crack in the leather had not let in a little air and light. The three boys crept in there and were silent for a long time. At last Huldrich said, "I wish father was at home again."

"So do I," said Witikind.

"We do not know but that he may be still alive," added Huldrich, "and kept a prisoner in the giant's castle."

"Let us go and set him free," cried Tapfer.

"How?" said the other two boys.

"Oh, we would do it. We will all three go there and fight the giant," said Tapfer.

And they all began talking of what they would do, when Huldrich said:

"But if we go, who will take care of our sisters and the little ones?" Then they all stopped, for not one of them wanted to be left behind. At last Huldrich said, "Tapfer, you ought to go, because you are the biggest and strongest. And I think father would say that I ought to remain behind, because I am the next biggest and strongest."

"You are a good fellow, Huldrich," replied Tapfer, "for I know you want to go as much as any of us. But so let it be settled, for I think you are right."

"And we two will start to-morrow morning," said Witikind.

"No," said Tapfer, "to-morrow we must get everything ready, and the day after we will start."

They agreed to tell nobody but Guta what they were going to do. Guta approved of their plan, and she made them a knapsack to carry some food for their journey. Tapfer went out into the forest and brought home a quantity of wood for Nurse to use while he was away. Huldrich sharpened the old knife so as to make it fit for use again, and he put a handle to the broken point, and gave it to Witikind to take with him. Tapfer had a small hatchet for cutting wood ; so now they were each armed with a weapon. Witikind spent the day in the forest, and came home laden with a hare, three rabbits, two moorhens, and a wild duck. All these Guta hung up in the larder except the wild duck. The boys determined to take it with them for the journey, so they lighted a fire in the garden and roasted it there, and some potatoes as well, for they were afraid to ask nurse for any bread.

The next morning they were up before daybreak. Tapfer carried the knapsack on his back with the food packed in it, and took his hatchet in his hand ; Witikind stuck the knife into his belt, and they started for Giant Groszfusz's castle. Huldrich and Guta went a little way with them through the forest, and then parted from them with many good wishes, and the two boys marched on alone.

They made their way through the pine trees until they came to a place where they knew there was a pass by which they could cross over the mountains into Giant Groszfusz's valley. They began to climb the mountain side, but it was so steep and the sun so hot, that Witikind was very glad when they sat down at noonday by a little stream to rest and dine. They found the cold duck and potatoes very refreshing, but they did not eat a great deal, because, as Witikind said, they must keep enough to make them strong to-morrow to fight the giant.

They were still working their way up the mountain side when the sun set and night came on. They knew that they

should have to spend a night on the road, and Guta had rolled
up a small blanket for them and tied it to the top of the knapsack.   So the two boys chose a sheltered place and lay down
close together, wrapping the blanket round them, and were so
tired that they immediately fell fast asleep.

The rising sun was making the snowy mountain tops look
like silver when Witikind woke next morning. He felt very
stiff and cramped, and for a moment wondered where he was,
and what was become of his little bed in the toe of the big
shoe.   Then he remembered all about it, and Tapfer starting
up at the same time, they refreshed themselves with a dip in
the stream and their breakfast, and started off again.   Three
hours' hard climbing brought them to the top, and before long
they could see below them in the valley a stone building that
must be the giant's castle.   The sight of this made them so
eager to get on that they raced down the hill, dropping from
rock to rock and sliding down the grassy slopes, so that by
mid-day they were at the bottom of the valley, and soon
afterwards drew near to the castle itself.

They came up to it very cautiously, for fear the giant should
look out and see them, and began peeping about to find some
way of getting in. But the great oak door was barred and
bolted, and the windows all too high for them to reach.
While they were standing under one of the windows, they
heard the giant's voice like the roar of a bull inside. Who
could he be speaking to? "Perhaps it is to our father," said
Tapfer.

"Brother, if you will roll up this great stone and stand on

it, and let me stand on your shoulder," said Witikind, " I think I could see in."

Tapfer did so ; and Witikind found that he was just able to peep over the stone window-sill. He saw a large room with an enormous fire burning in it, and by the fire sat Giant Groszfusz in an arm-chair, under which you might have built a cottage. Before him stood a dish as big as a sitz-bath, out of which he was eating with a spoon that would hold as much as a soup tureen.

"Slave! bring me my beer!" roared the giant. And the boys' father came forward, dragging a pewter pot as big as a wash-tub, filled to the brim with beer. When Witikind saw that, he was so angry that he gave a jump forward, and would have fallen to the ground if Tapfer had not caught him.

Soon after they heard the giant moving about, and presently out he came with his great club in his hand. Tapfer and Witikind watched him go past, crouched behind the stone.

Now was their time to get into the castle. Tapfer lifted Witikind up to the window again, and he scrambled in ; and seeing a rope lying near him, he tied it to one of the window bars and flung the end down to Tapfer, who soon drew himself up by it with his strong arms.

But where was their father? They went all over the castle, they opened every door and peeped into every corner ; no one was to be found. Then they began to shout, louder and louder, "Father! father!" Still there was no sound until, as they came into the kitchen again, they thought they heard a faint voice answering from under the floor.

"There is a trap-door in the corner," cried Witikind.

They ran to it, but it was locked and they could not lift it.

"Who calls me?" said their father's voice from underneath.

"It is we, father, your boys Tapfer and Witikind. We are come to fetch you home. Do you know where the key of the trap-door is kept?"

"The giant keeps it always hanging round his waist," replied their father. "But do not stay here, boys; do not let the giant get you."

"Never fear, father," said Tapfer, "we will be very careful."

And as he spoke, the room shook with the giant's tread as he came home from his walk; and the two boys scuttled away up-stairs as fast as they could scamper, and looked about for a place to hide in. There was a pair of new boots of the giant's standing under his bed, and the boys thought they should feel quite at home in one of these, after living so long in one of his old shoes. So in they scrambled, pulling themselves up by one of the laces; and then they began to consult what to do next.

They agreed that they must wait till the giant went to bed, and then steal the key and get their father out by night; for even Tapfer allowed that the giant was too big and his own axe too small to think of fighting him.

He must go down, he said, and see what the key was like and what it was tied on with, so as to know it again in a moment. So when they heard the giant at his supper, Tapfer crept softly down stairs, and peeped through the crack of the door while Witikind waited on the top of the boot to help him in again quickly if he had to run and hide.

The giant was very merry over his supper, boasting how he was going to kill a whole village to-morrow, and bring home a pocketful of fat children to eat. Tapfer was as indignant as Witikind had been to see how the giant ordered his father about, but he comforted himself with thinking that this was the last time. As soon as the giant had finished, and was locking the trap-door over his father again, Tapfer crept safely back to the boot.

Presently the giant came up to bed.

" Ho, ho," said he, sniffing about, "the rats have got into my castle again. I smell you, you rascals, I smell you !" I must send to my cousin in Africa to let me have a few tigers to keep in my castle ; they will soon eat them up. Humph, humph," he went on, still sniffing about, " I wonder where their hole is." And he began hunting behind the boxes and under the bed, and even moved the boot in which the boys were hiding.

They were terribly frightened, but they did not move, and before long the giant gave up hunting for the supposed rat-hole and went to bed.

The boys waited until the giant began to snore. Then they came softly out and began looking about by the light of the moon to see where the giant had put down his key. It was not on the table, nor with his clothes. And when a ray of moonlight fell on the giant himself, behold there lay the key with his thumb stuck through the handle, and a cord to which

it was tied twisted round his wrist.   It would be impossible
to take it away without waking him.

The two boys looked at one another in dismay.   What was
to be done now ?

"I will climb on to the bed and cut his throat with my
hatchet," said Tapfer.

"No, brother, do not try," said Witikind; "for his beard is
all over his throat, so that you cannot get at it, and before
you could kill him he would wake and kill you.   But listen, I
have a plan.   Do you remember how Jack the Giant-killer
slew the Cornish giant ?"

"Yes; by digging a pit and covering it over with branches,"
whispered Tapfer in reply.   "But we have no time to dig pits."

"I know that," said Witikind; "but don't you remember
the great tank of beer that we saw in the castle, underneath
that long passage ? Suppose we were to cut some of the floor
of the passage nearly through, and then get the giant to run
along it.   Down he would go into his beer and be drowned.
What do you think of that plan ?"

Tapfer thought it would do capitally, and they went at once
to the passage and began cutting away at the boards, Tapfer
with his hatchet, and Witikind with his knife-point, which did
something, although it certainly could not do much.

"It is very dark," said Tapfer presently.   I think the moon
must be setting.   I cannot see to work fast enough."

"I will get a light," said Witikind.   He had noticed a great
oil-flask in the kitchen, so he ran and pulled several threads
out of the giant's great dish-cloth, twisted them together,

poked all but an inch or two down into the flask, and then lighted the end at the fire. It burned capitally, and by the light of this make-shift lamp the work went on much faster. Tapfer grew so eager over it, and made such a noise with his hatchet once, that the giant gave a great snort and turned over in bed. This frightened them very much, and they dared not begin to work again until they heard him snoring as soundly as ever.

The boys were so anxious to set free their father, and so much afraid of the giant's hearing them, that they forgot to feel either sleepy or hungry, and worked on till the sun rose, and the giant rolled out of bed with a tremendous yawn. As he never washed himself, his dressing did not take long, and presently they heard him coming stump, stump, down the stairs, like half-a-dozen elephants all marching together. Then the boys ran and hid themselves behind the passage door as they had agreed to do. And Tapfer climbed up by means of a rope which Witikind had untied from the giant's last packet of brown sugar, and stood on the door-handle with his hatchet in his hand. As the giant passed through to fetch his morning draught of beer, Tapfer made a cut with his hatchet at the cord round the giant's wrist to which the trap-door key was hung. Down fell the key, and round turned the giant with a yell to seize Tapfer. But he swung himself quickly behind the door with his rope, while Witikind ran forward, and danced and shouted in front of the giant, flourishing his little knife-end.

"Ho, ho, it was you, was it, you whipper-snapper!" roared

Groszfusz. But as he stooped to pick him up, Witikind darted
lightly away to the other end of the passage. The giant
came lumbering after, but when he reached the middle of the
passage, crack went the boards, down tumbled Giant Groszfusz
with a crash that shook the earth for seven miles round, and
was drowned in his own beer-tank.

Witikind scrambled back across the broken planks and
beam-ends, and the two brothers hugged one another for joy.
Then they picked up the great key and ran to the trap-door.
Their father had heard the crash of the giant's fall, and he
called out, " Are you safe, my children ?"

" Safe and sound, father," cried they ; "and the giant is
dead, and we are come to bring you out."

The key was so heavy, that when they had put into its hole
they could by no means get it to turn until they put the
giant's ivory penholder, made out of an elephant's tusk,
through the handle, and so pushed it round between them.
Then their father shoved up the door from underneath, and
they quickly thrust the great salt-cellar under as a wedge
while he crept out, pale and thin with long imprisonment.

When they had kissed and hugged one another until they
were all out of breath, the boys suddenly discovered that they
had had no breakfast and were very hungry. So they hunted
among the giant's stores, and found enough to make a good
meal, and to fill the knapsack for their journey home.

It would be hard to say which were the most anxious to
get home, the boys or their father. So they determined to
begin their journey that very morning, although their father

was so weak that Tapfer gave Witikind the knapsack to carry, in order that he might support his father. It was still early when they left behind the dark walls of the giant's castle, Witikind marching in front with the well-filled knapsack, and with the great key stuck in his belt as a trophy; but often looking back as he climbed to offer a hand to his father, who followed with Tapfer's strong arm thrown round him to help him along the homeward path.

It was the evening of the fourth day after Tapfer and Witikind had left the old shoe on their bold adventure. Guta, accompanied as usual by several of the little ones, had come into the garden to call Huldrich in to supper.

"It will soon be dark," she said. "See, the snow mountains are beginning to take their rosy sunset colour. I wonder whether they will come home to-day."

"Ah," replied Huldrich, "I have been hoping so all day. I can think of nothing else. I do so long to know how they have sped, and whether they have found father there."

"Father! is father coming home?" asked one of the smallest boys, pulling at Guta's sleeve.

"Hush!" cried Huldrich, throwing down his spade. "I thought I heard—yes, that is Witikind's shout."

And at that moment Witikind appeared from among the trees, shouting and waving his cap over his head as a sign of victory. He had tried to wave the key, but it was too heavy.

"They are safe! Father is with them!" cried Huldrich and Guta. And they began running towards the forest, with the little ones running after them in a long string. In another moment their father was surrounded by his seventeen children ; and there was such a hugging and kissing and laughing and crying, that old nurse came running out of the shoe to see what was the matter, and dropped their last willow-pattern plate for joy at seeing her master again.

They did not go on living in the shoe. When government took possession of Giant Groszfusz's castle, it gave half the treasures that were found in it to the boys and their father because they had suffered so much from the giant and had conquered him so bravely. So there was plenty of money to build up their house again. They built it in the same spot, only it was still larger and more comfortable than the old one had been.

Now it was the village in their own parish that the giant had meant to go and destroy on the very day that Tapfer and Witikind had put an end to his cruel deeds. And when the villagers heard this, they all brought them presents to show their gratitude. The good old pastor gave them a cow, and the schoolmaster gave them a swarm of bees, and the other villagers brought tables and chairs and beds and sheets ; so the house was soon furnished. And the pastor's wife gave them a new tea set of white china with gold stars painted on it, which made nurse quite happy again.

"Who would have thought, Witikind," said Huldrich, on the day that they went into their new house, "that all this happiness would have come of your breaking the bread-knife ?"

" And of nurse's being put out and whipping us all ; do you

remember ?" replied Witikind. And taking hold of a little girl with one hand and a little boy with the other, he began to dance round and round while he sang :

> " There was an old woman who lived in a shoe,
> She had so many children she didn't know what to do ;
> She gave them some broth without any bread,
> She whipped them all soundly and sent them to bed."

And all the other children danced too, and their father came in and he danced too. And old nurse, who was no longer cross now that she had not too much to do, laughed as she sat and watched them.

So they all lived happily together in their new house. As for the old shoe, it was quite deserted, and it made a capital place for the little ones to go and play at hide and seek.

XVI.—A MONARCH'S DAUGHTER.

> " Once I was a monarch's daughter,
>   And sat on a lady's knee ;
> Now I am a lonely wanderer,
>   Sitting in the ivy tree,
> Crying, Hoo hoo hoo, hoo hoo hoo,
>   Hoo hoo hoo, my feet are cold !
> Pity me, for here you see me
>   Persecuted, poor and old."

A YOUNG prince was once walking with a nobleman who was his constant companion, in a thick wood near his father's palace. Evening was coming on, and as they passed an old hollow oak tree nearly hidden in the ivy that grew up round it, the prince was startled by the melancholy cry of an owl.

" Tu whoo, tu whoo !" it said ;

> " Once I was a monarch's daughter,
>   And sat on a lady's knee ;
> Now I am a lonely wanderer,
>   Sitting in the ivy-tree,
> Crying, Hoo hoo hoo, hoo hoo hoo,
>   Hoo hoo hoo, my feet are cold !
> Pity me, for here you see me
>   Persecuted, poor and old."

" Hark !" said the prince, " did you hear what that owl was

A MONARCH'S DAUGHTER.

saying ? How mournful it was : it has made me feel quite sad."

" What the owl was saying !" replied the young nobleman who was with him ; "your royal highness must be joking. I only heard the owl say Tu whoo, like every other owl. But if it makes you sad, I will·soon put a stop to it."

" How ?" said the prince.

" By fetching my bow and arrow," answered his companion. " I am not a bad shot, as your royal highness knows, and a well-aimed arrow would soon stop that doleful hooting."

" Do not think of such a thing," said the prince. " I shall be very angry if you shoot the owl : it does no harm, poor creature. Come, it is getting chilly, let us go in."

All that night the prince could not get the owl's mournful " Hoo hoo hoo " out of his head. So the next day he determined to find the owl, and went out to the wood again ; but this time without his companion. As he came near the hollow tree, he heard the owl repeating the same melancholy song.

" Poor creature," thought the prince, " perhaps it is hurt." And climbing up through the ivy he peeped into the hollow tree. There sat a large white owl. But instead of flying away, or hissing and pecking at him, as a common owl would have done, it sat still and stared at him with its great sad eyes.

It looked so strange that the prince felt half inclined to slip down again. However, he was ashamed to be afraid of an owl, so he said, " Owl, why are you so sad ?"

The owl replied,

> " Once I was a monarch's daughter,
>   And sat on a lady's knee ;
> But when I lost my father
>   A cousin took charge of me.
> Aud because my people loved me,
>   And because I was fair to see,
> My jealous cousin has made me
>   An owl in the ivy tree,
> Crying, Hoo hoo hoo, hoo hoo hoo,
>   Hoo hoo hoo, my feet are cold !
> Pity me, for here you see me,
>   Persecuted, poor and old."

"Poor old owl !" said the prince.   "Tell me about it, and I will try to help you."

And the owl said,

> " Strange the tale, and hard the task :
>   Will you do whate'er I ask ?"

"Yes, if I can," said the prince.

And the owl answered again :

> " When the moon is shining low,
>   You must wander out alone :
> You must pluck the flowers that grow
>   Round a mossy, carven stone.
> Steep in wine, and then divide it
>   Into portions three :
> A third to drink, a third to keep,
>   A third to give to me."

"That does not sound very difficult," said the prince. "And shall I drink my third, as soon as I have steeped the flowers ?"

> " He that sips
> With sullied lips
> His doom has quaffed.
> Lip that's pure
> May endure
> The dangerous draught,"

replied the owl.

> " Mighty is the potion's power,
> Keep it for the fated hour."

The prince began to consider whether his lips had ever been sullied by an untruthful or unjust word. " Nay then," said he, " I shall certainly bring it all to you. But owl, why do you always answer in this odd, mysterious way?"

The owl still looking sadly at him, replied :

> " Fate, not choice,
> Guides my voice
> Ask no more, go forth and do :
> Tu whit, tu whoo !"

So that night, when the crescent moon had sunk low in the west, the prince went forth to seek for the magic herb by that uncertain light. And as he walked, he suddenly entered a moonlit glen, and before him lay what had once been the statue of a nymph, but it was thrown down and broken and moss-covered. Over the carved stone face there grew a plant whose small starry flowers shone like silver in the moonbeams. The prince immediately gathered it, and as he walked home he thought he heard a rustle of wings as though the owl were flying near him.

The next day, having poured his magic drink into three

silver flasks, he went out to the ivy tree. There sat the owl as before. The prince told her what he had done. "And what shall I do next to serve you?" he asked.

The owl said,

> " Will you serve me? Come then, where
> Reigns the lady false and fair.
>
> But beware—
>
> Her softest smile
> Is full of guile :
> If thou art firm 'gainst flattery,
> Prince, arise and follow me."

The prince felt very curious to see the end of this adventure, so he said, " I am not afraid of being flattered, and if you will show me the way I am ready to go with you."

And the owl flew out of the tree and answered,

> " If thou wilt keep thy promise true,
> Mount and away—tu whit tu whoo !"

Then the prince mounted his horse, and the owl flew by his side, and they travelled for three nights, sleeping by day and journeying by night. Early in the morning after the third night's journey, they came to the end of the dominions of the prince's father. And across the border there rode to meet them a band of gaily dressed horsemen, with fifes and trumpets. The owl tried to speak, but her voice was lost in the sound of the music, and the prince spurred merrily on. When he came up to them they all bowed low, and their captain said,

"The great Queen Lisonja, sovereign of this land, has sent

us to greet your royal highness, and to entreat you to consider her palace yours, if you will deign to enter it."

"She is very kind," said the prince, "but I am come on an errand which I wish to do with all speed, and to return home without delay."

"The great Queen Lisonja knows your errand, O prince, and she bids us say that if you will confide in her, she will rejoice to carry out your wishes."

As the captain spoke, there was a blast of trumpets, and a queen in glittering robes rode up followed by her court. She looked so fair and smiling that the prince thought, "Certainly this cannot be the false cousin who enchanted my owl." And as she was getting down to greet him, he ran forward and kissed her hand. But she would hardly let him do so, and she told him how much she had heard of him, of his beauty and his valour and his wisdom ; but that now she came to see him she perceived that people had not praised him half enough.

And the young prince blushed for pleasure ; and he went back with Queen Lisonja to her stately palace, listening to her sweet sayings, and forgot all about his poor owl, who had never said such fine things to him.

Lisonja prepared a splendid feast in his honour, and it was not till it was nearly over that the prince remembered his errand, and said that he must be going.

"Ah," said Lisonja, "I see your kind, generous heart has been touched by that owl's story. But with your quick wit, you must have perceived that the poor thing is crazy : not half of her story is true.   Besides, it was all her own fault, as such things mostly are.   That enchanted wine that she gave you—your royal highness has not drunk any I hope?"

" No, not yet," said the prince.

"Ah, l am glad of that," said Lisonja.   " The poor foolish owl believes it to be poison.   It is not quite so bad as that, but it might disagree with you very much; let me strongly advise you to fling it away."

" I cannot think that she believes it to be poison," said the prince, " for she said some of it is for herself.   At any rate, I undertook the adventure, and I shall keep my promise."

"Spoken like your noble, valorous self!" cried Lisonja, "But not to-night, I cannot let my sweet prince go to-night. Your fair cheek is wan for lack of sleep; honour me by reposing this night in my poor palace."

So the prince stayed ; and he slept so soundly that he did not hear the melancholy " Hoo hoo hoo" of the owl as she circled vainly round the palace.

The next day Queen Lisonja must take the prince to see her gardens, and then she must have his portrait painted for her to keep, and so on from day to day, until a week had slipped away, and still the poor white owl was forgotten.

The prince was indeed so charmed with Lisonja's graces that he began to persuade himself that the owl really was half crazy and half malicious in her efforts to be righted again from the wrongs which she complained of.   "And it is asking too much, as Lisonja says," thought the prince, "to expect a prince like me to devote my life to an old owl." He did not, however, throw away the enchanted wine, as Lisonja often urged him to do, and he always intended to see the owl again, and beg her to explain herself better. But somehow the time never came, for what with concerts and feasts and dances, his nights were as fully occupied as his days : and what chance had the owl to be heard, even if she should venture into all that noise and light and bustle ?

One morning the prince came home from bathing earlier than usual, and instead of going into the grand sitting-room set apart for him, he went into an arbour in the garden. This arbour was so placed that he could see into a drawing-room where Lisonja and some of her ladies were sitting, and for some time he amused himself with watching Lisonja playing with a little dog which she seemed to be very fond of. But presently he grew troublesome, as little dogs will when they are too much romped with, and when she tried to quiet him he would not be quiet. One of the ladies tried to turn him out, but he would not go. Then the prince saw Lisonja get up and offer him a biscuit. Of course the little dog ran up to get it, and she led him to the door, still holding out the biscuit. Then instead of the biscuit she gave the little dog a kick that sent him whining out, and shut the door in his face. And she and all her ladies laughed, but the prince felt very angry. "I do not like her at all," thought he, "she is cruel and false. If she could cheat the poor dog like that, she may be cheating me ; and if she is unkind to him, she may have been unkind to my poor white owl." And he went to his room, and began walking up and down in a very disturbed state of mind.

Before he had made up his mind what to do, they came to tell him that his horse was at the door, and that Queen Lisonja begged him to come out hunting with her. Her soft speeches were disagreeable to him now, and he parted from her as soon as he could, and rode away by himself.

As he rode along he thought he heard a faint cry of an owl from a neighbouring thicket. He went to it, and there at the bottom of an old dry well, whose sides had fallen in and were covered with fern, he saw his white owl lying, almost too weak to move.

She turned her mournful eyes to his as he stooped over her, and said :

> " O Prince most faithless, most untrue !
> Who promised fair, but did not do—
> Tu whoo ! tu whoo !"

The prince was so sorry that he did not know what to say, but he took the owl in his cloak and rode gently back with her to his room, and there recovered her with food and gentle words, until she was able to speak to him again.

"I will not fail you this time, dear owl," he said. "Only let me serve you again, and I will do anything for you that you ask."

And the owl replied,

> " Now is come the fated hour ;
> Try the wondrous potion's power."

Meanwhile Lisonja and her attendants were riding up and

down over the country, looking for the prince. At last they came home without him ; and very soon afterwards a page knocked at the prince's door with a message from Lisonja, begging him to come out and speak to her, that she might be sure he was not ill or hurt.

"I will come at once," said the prince, who had agreed with the owl what he was to do.

"Oh, my sweet prince, my noble friend !" cried Lisonja, as he came into the room, "how terrified I have been for you ! how my heart——"

"Flatterer !" interrupted the prince. "Where is the Princess Verdadera, whom her dying father intrusted to your care ?"

Lisonja looked startled for a moment, but answered, "Oh, I see that crazy old owl has been with you again. Surely you do not believe her. I have told you the real state of the case, and how the wrongs she fancies are all her own fault. Your clear judgment, my prince——"

"If what you have told me is the truth, you will not hesitate to drink this," cried the prince, presenting her with one of the silver flasks. At the same moment the white owl flew into the room.

Lisonja fell down on her knees. "Oh, send her away !" she cried. "She wants to take away my character—she is going to poison me—O noble prince !——"

But the prince sprinkled on her a few drops from the flask, and so great was their magic power that Lisonja could no longer resist, but was forced to drink. The moment the enchanted draught touched her lips sullied with falsehood and flattery, she sank down with a scream, and behold, instead of the richly-robed queen, a hideous snake lay wriggling on the steps of the throne. And all her attendants turned into snakes, writhing and coiling around her.

Now it was the prince's turn to drink ; but he, seeing the terrible effect it had had on the false Lisonja, shrank from putting the flask to his lips. Then the snakes rose up hissing to attack him, and the owl cried out,

> " Pause not to think—
> Drink, O drink !"

And he drank. There was no change in his appearance, except that his form grew more upright and his brow more open, and the snakes cowered and shrank and fled away from before him. But the prince stood covered with shame and dismay, for the magic draught seemed to have opened his eyes so that he saw what he really was : how silly and conceited in listening to Lisonja's flatteries, how thoughtlessly cruel to the owl, how idly he was spending his whole life in useless amusements, how careless of his people whom he ought to be learning how to govern aright, how selfish in everything.

"O owl," he cried, "I have been behaving very badly. I am not fit—I do not deserve to help you any more !"

But where was the owl ? The third silver flask lay empty on the table, and beside it stood, not the white owl, but a lovely white-robed princess with clear, beautiful eyes, and such a loving smile on her face that the prince knelt down and would have kissed the hem of her robe.

But she raised him up and said, "Your white owl thanks you, prince, for having set her free from her enchanted shape, and her tongue from speaking in riddles. By your aid, I am the Princess Verdadera again, and queen of all this land. Rise up and tell me what I can do to prove my gratitude."

"Alas!" said the prince, "I have done nothing to deserve it. I have behaved so ill to you that I cannot tell why the magic draught has not done the same to me as it did to Lisonja."

"Because," replied Verdadera, "although you have been thoughtless, you have not been false."

"What is the wonderful herb that it is made from, then?" asked the prince.

"That little plant with the white starry flower is the herb of truth," said Princess Verdadera. "We will keep some always by us, and then we need fear neither self-deceit nor flattery."

"Ah, Verdadera," said the prince, "if I may dare to hope that you will still trust me, I will try never to be vain and thoughtless again."

As he spoke, all the good old courtiers of the times of Verdadera's father, having heard that their own princess was come back again, crowded into the palace court to welcome her. And the princess allowed the prince to lead her forward, and presented him to her people as her deliverer. Then she turned to him and said :

"To-morrow we will ride to the king your father's court, and ask his blessing on our marriage. Then we will return and govern our people with the rule of love and truth."

So they rode over the hills and through the forests to the court of the prince's father. And all the city came out to meet them, with the young nobleman, the prince's old companion, among the first. He little thought, while he looked at the beautiful princess, that he had once very much wished to shoot her.

As they passed the old ivy-covered tree in the palace grounds, Verdadera turned smiling to the prince, and sang :

> " Once I was a lonely wanderer,
>   Sitting in the ivy tree :
> Now a happy maiden, riding
>   With the Prince that set me free ;
> Singing, Joy joy joy, joy joy joy,
>   O my heart is full of glee !
> Full of love for those around me,
>   Most of all for him who found me
> Sitting in the ivy tree."

But I never could learn that Lisonja and her attendant snakes have been killed, so every one must take care to have a good supply of the herb of truth always by them.

THE END.

LONDON : PRINTED BY W. CLOWES AND SONS, STAMFORD STREET AND CHARING CROSS

9 783744 767583